BULLET CATCH SHOWDOWN

Stage magician Malachi Muldoon is the world's most dangerous practitioner of the arcane arts with his performance of the notorious bullet catch. His show in Bear Creek draws the interest of Adam Clements and Deputy Hayward Knight. While Clements is keen to join Malachi on stage and become part of his act, Hayward is out to try and solve a mystery: it seems that, wherever Malachi Muldoon performs, a trail of bodies is left behind . . .

I. J. PARNHAM

BULLET CATCH SHOWDOWN

Complete and Unabridged

LINFORD
Leicester

First published in Great Britain in 2014 by
Robert Hale Limited
London

First Linford Edition
published 2017
by arrangement with
Robert Hale
an imprint of
The Crowood Press
Wiltshire

A catalogue record for this book is available
from the British Library.

ISBN 978–1–4448–3488–8

Published by
F. A. Thorpe (Publishing)
Anstey, Leicestershire

Set by Words & Graphics Ltd.
Anstey, Leicestershire
Printed and bound in Great Britain by
T. J. International Ltd., Padstow, Cornwall

This book is printed on acid-free paper

1

'It's a trick,' Adam Clements said.

'Of course it is,' Lucy said with an excited giggle. 'That's why it's called a magic show.'

Adam uttered an exasperated sigh and settled down in his chair to try to work out how Malachi Muldoon, the world's most dangerous practitioner of the arcane arts, would next deceive his gullible audience.

He'd already poured scorn on Malachi's first trick in which he'd opened a safe that had been empty only to find it was now full of gold and jewels. Malachi had been so shocked by the unexpected appearance he'd slammed the door shut and when he'd reopened it a moment later, his female assistant Florence was inside dressed in a gaudy and barely decent costume.

The audience applauded, but Adam

noted that they found her a more interesting sight than the treasure, so they didn't watch the safe closely. So he hadn't been impressed when Malachi moved the safe aside revealing a suspicious square shape on the stage that suggested a trapdoor.

That observation hadn't impressed Lucy, and Adam had been even less impressed with the card trick. Malachi had used a knife to spear one of the playing cards Florence had held up, and this card turned out to be the same card that earlier a member of the audience had selected.

Adam reckoned Malachi had two packs of cards and someone had told him which card had been chosen. Lucy hadn't taken that revelation well either and already he was wishing that for his first night in a new town he'd sought out a saloon girl who hadn't wanted to go to the show.

'And now for your edification and delight,' Malachi announced from the front of the stage while looking along the first row of the excited audience, 'I will perform the most dangerous act you'll ever witness in your entire lives.'

The audience cheered in anticipation, but an inebriated man on the front row stood up and gestured at the stage.

'If you want real danger, spend a Saturday night in Bear Creek,' he shouted while struggling to remain upright.

Appreciative laughter rang out while Malachi stared at the man pensively.

'Eight legendary performers have died demonstrating the death-defying, the breathtaking, the notorious bullet catch.'

'Eight deaths.' The man shrugged. 'Still sounds like a typical Saturday night in Bear Creek!'

The audience roared with laughter, forcing Malachi to parade in a circle while he waited for order to return.

'In that case, perhaps you'd like to come up here and help me with my act,' he said when the noise had subsided. 'You can carry out the death-defying part.'

Laughter rang out along with catcalls

encouraging the heckler to go up on stage, making Adam nod knowingly. He leaned towards Lucy.

'That man's working with Malachi,' he said. 'He's part of the act.'

'No he's not,' Lucy snapped. 'And stop spoiling it for me.'

Adam sat back waiting to be proved right, but to his disappointment, and Lucy's glee, the heckler bowed acknowledging he'd been bettered and sat back down. After the merriment of the lively exchange, everyone sat quietly as Malachi set up his next act.

Florence dragged a hoop on a pole on to the stage. Then she pushed the pole around so everyone could see the glass in the hoop and the knotted rope that surrounded the glass like a hangman's noose.

Malachi paced out exact measurements across the stage until he found two spots at opposite ends that he deemed to be suitable and which he marked with crosses. Then he did the same precise pacing out to position the hoop in the centre of the stage between the two marks.

He didn't explain why the positioning was important, but his act had enraptured everyone and so the audience waited quietly for him to be ready.

Finally, Florence brought out a shining Peacemaker on a silver tray after which Malachi beckoned for a member of the audience to come up and examine the gun.

Adam was leaning over to Lucy to make the point that this person would be the heckler when, to a round of applause, Sheriff Washington clambered up on to the stage. His participation had clearly been arranged beforehand as he and Malachi chatted amiably until Malachi drew him forward to face the audience.

'Can you confirm this is your Peacemaker?' Malachi asked, as Florence held up the tray.

'Sure is,' Washington said, addressing the audience. 'And it's the cleanest it's ever been.'

The heckler shouted something, but his speech was slurred and Adam couldn't hear what he said. This time his interjection wasn't received as enthusiastically as before and the audience beckoned him to be quiet.

'And can you confirm your gun is loaded?'

Florence opened the cylinder letting Washington peer at the chambers.

'Sure can.'

'And finally, will you accept my solemn statement that I make here before all these good people that if my death-defying act goes awry and I am killed here tonight on this very stage, no crime will have been committed?'

'I will,' Washington said with a sombre tone, after which Florence led him to the back of the stage to stand behind the hoop.

Malachi lowered his head and took deep breaths before he paced to his mark at the side of the stage. When he was in position, a second man emerged from the back of the stage and stood on the other mark so that he faced Malachi through the glass hoop.

This man wore a long, black cloak and below his wide hat a mask covered his face so only his eyes could be seen through the two holes in the mask. Florence brought over the tray and with due gravity the masked man took the Peacemaker before she scurried back to join Sheriff Washington.

She rummaged behind her and located a brand, which she lit, although her hand shook and she required several attempts. When her nervous fumbling made several people laugh, Malachi raised a hand calling for quiet.

'As I don't want Sheriff Washington to complete his promise, I need silence,' he said. He coughed and lowered his tone. 'But in case I don't defy death, my killer is wearing a mask to ensure his identity will never become known.'

In a room that had become so silent Adam could hear his own heartbeat, the masked man raised the gun while Malachi settled his stance and adopted a pose with his head jutting forward and his arms thrust backwards.

Florence put the brand to the hoop and the rope must have been soaked in oil as it burst into flame.

Adam was close to the stage and so he had to look from side to side to watch both the masked man and Malachi. He also watched Florence, Sheriff Washington, and the burning hoop, feeling unsure about who or what he should watch so he could work out how the trick was performed.

He was peering at Florence, noting she was tapping a finger against the plate on which the gun had rested earlier, when the masked man fired.

The glass cracked and fell from the hoop. The sudden sounds made Adam jump in his seat, not that he needed to be embarrassed as everyone else leapt to their feet.

He had to crane his neck to see what had happened through the mass of people who were also craning their necks. When he saw that Malachi had fallen over and he was lying motionless on his side, he wished he hadn't looked.

'What's happening?' Lucy asked, jumping on the spot as she failed to see over the heads before her.

'You don't want to see . . . ' Adam trailed off when Malachi twitched and got to his knees.

Applause erupted as Malachi raised a hand to confirm he was fine. Then Florence walked over to him gingerly, taking care to avoid the glass the masked man's bullet had shattered.

She held out the plate and, after shaking his head vigorously as if shrugging off a blow, Malachi turned to the audience and smiled. In the gap between his upper and lower teeth, there was clearly an object. Then he jerked his head forward and spat out a bullet on to the plate.

As cheering rose up from every corner of the room, Sheriff Washington came over to inspect the slug. His incredulous expression told the audience everything they needed to know.

Malachi had caught the bullet in his teeth.

'So, how did he do that?' Lucy said, as the audience sat down.

'It's a trick,' Adam said. He considered her aggrieved expression and blurted out his best guess. 'Malachi had already put a bullet in his mouth and when the flames around the hoop shattered the glass, the masked man fired over Malachi's head.'

'I don't think so.' She pouted. 'I think he caught the bullet with his teeth.'

She glared at him, and although admitting he'd been impressed would help him enjoy the rest of the evening, he couldn't bring himself to agree.

'And now after my brush with seemingly certain death,' Malachi announced to his enthralled audience before Adam could reply, 'I'll end my performance here tonight by turning my attention on to you, my good friends. I intend to make one of you disappear. Do I have a volunteer?'

'Make him disappear,' a man shouted on the front row while pointing at the drunken heckler.

To a round of growing support, the heckler stood up, pleasing Adam as he'd identified him earlier as being in Malachi's employ. He tapped Lucy's arm, but she batted him away.

With everyone shouting encouragement, the heckler turned to the stage. Unfortunately, he was so inebriated he stumbled into another man, knocking him over. Then he tripped over another man's legs and went sprawling over several people.

While he extricated himself, raucous laughter rang out relieving the tension of the last few minutes. Then, when he gained his feet, he walked by the steps leading up to the stage and he had to be directed back to them where he took several attempts to work out how to climb up.

By the time the heckler reached the stage Malachi was glowering and, when Florence directed him to his position, he lunged for her. She avoided his grasping hands with a deft wiggle, but the movement unbalanced him and he fell forwards like a toppled tree on to the stage.

Then he rolled off it and crashed into a man who had been working his way back to his seat. While people crowded in to check they were unharmed and others stood up asking to volunteer in his place, Malachi stood over the spot where the heckler had fallen shaking his head.

Adam was still working out how this turn of events fitted into his theory when Lucy dragged him to his feet.

'Make him disappear,' Lucy screeched, her voice cutting through the hubbub. 'Then I won't have to listen to any more of his prattle.'

Her loud comment drew attention to Adam and people started shouting for Malachi to pick him. For his part, Malachi watched the heckler, who was tussling with the man who had broken his fall, until the audience's reaction made him look at Adam followed by several other people who had been picked out.

Malachi raised a hand and pointed a

finger straight up, holding the pose until he had quiet. Then he lowered the hand and the finger pointed at Adam.

'I'll make him disappear,' he said, to a round of applause. 'And later, if his delightful escort consents, I'll bring him back.'

Lucy squealed and waved as she enjoyed the attention. With her ignoring him, Adam made his way to the stage.

At the steps, he waited while Sheriff Washington and his deputy instilled calm by dragging the heckler away. Then, on the stage, he struggled to look at a large number of people who were looking at him, so he faced Malachi, who was peering at him intently.

'I'm Adam Clements,' he said, although he hadn't been asked. 'And that's Lucy . . . I don't know her second name.'

He knew he was babbling, but his comment raised a laugh. When several men shouted out Lucy's full name along with how much she charged, Malachi beckoned Florence to approach.

13

The next few minutes passed in a blur. Adam tried to watch everything that happened, but standing on stage made him feel self-conscious and so he let Florence lead him around meekly.

After much parading around the stage, he found himself standing in the black box that had been fashioned to resemble a safe and from which Florence had magically appeared earlier.

Malachi reached in and shook his hand while favouring him with a wink. Then he slammed the door shut leaving Adam bracing himself for whatever happened next.

When all he heard was Malachi explaining how he was the only man who knew the mystical art of making men disappear and then reappear, he looked around the box.

He saw nothing untoward and so he felt the door, which made him realize his hand was cold. He opened his hand and silver flashed before dropping from view.

Bemused, he dropped to his knees to

find a silver dollar spinning to a halt on the base. When he cast his mind back, he now reckoned he'd felt something cold on his palm when Malachi had shaken his hand.

He was still wondering why Malachi had given him money when a small door at the back he hadn't noticed before dropped open and Florence peered in. She put a finger to her lips. Then she gestured, encouraging him to crawl away.

'You want me to follow you?' he whispered.

'Of course,' she said with a wink that was slower and more intriguing than Malachi's. 'How else is he going to make you disappear?'

'I don't know,' Adam murmured.

'In that case, just remember this.' She took his hand and tugged. 'It's a trick.'

2

'So how did Malachi catch the bullet?' Deputy Hayward Knight asked when Sheriff Washington had settled down in his chair in the law office.

'We've been dealing with this one,' Washington said, signifying Derrick Fox, the drunken heckler Hayward had dumped on a chair. 'So I've not been thinking about Malachi Muldoon.'

Hayward laughed at Washington's evasive answer and moved over to consider the almost comatose prisoner.

'You want me to lock him in a cell?'

'No. Let him sit there until he wakes up. Then he can crawl back into the gutter.'

'You're generous tonight. You must have enjoyed Malachi's show.'

Washington shrugged, again passing up the opportunity to talk about what he'd seen on stage.

'Derrick was only boisterous, so we can't waste time on him when we've got a more serious matter to worry about.' Washington raised an eyebrow, implying the seriousness of the situation before he explained. 'While we were at the show, I heard the rumour that Ralston Hope's returned.'

Hayward had come to Bear Creek a year after Ralston had been run out of town, so it took him a moment to recall the details. When he did, he winced and it may have been a coincidence but Derrick jerked and sat upright on his chair.

'What you bring me here for?' he murmured, peering around blearily.

Hayward waved at him to be quiet and drew Washington aside.

'That has to be wrong,' he said. 'Ralston would never return.'

'Men like Ralston don't think like others do.'

Hayward tipped back his hat as he contemplated the unwelcome situations the next few days might bring.

'Unfinished business or looking to stir up old hatreds?'

'It could be both.' Washington dragged Derrick to his feet before beckoning Hayward to join him in leaving. 'But unfortunately for Ralston I'm not a patient man, so we won't wait for him to let us know.'

* ★ *

'How will Malachi make me reappear?' Adam asked when he'd crawled off the stage.

'He's a magician,' Florence said with a smile. 'He'll magic you back.'

Adam furrowed his brow, but her only response was to laugh and head on to the stage where she paraded around the now empty safe.

From the side of the stage, Adam could now see the mirror that had been positioned behind the safe to hide his escape. And when she moved the mirror, he noted how her constant movement and bright costume drew the eye, presumably to distract the audience from noticing other elements of the trick.

'What Malachi does is even more impressive when you can see how it's done,' a man said behind him.

Adam turned to find the cloaked man had joined him, although he'd removed his mask. He introduced himself as Severin O'Hara.

'I knew it was a trick,' Adam said. When Severin smiled, he shrugged. 'Well, of course it is, but I thought Florence had sneaked into the safe through a trapdoor. Now I can see how she got there.'

'You think you can see, but don't be so sure. Malachi is the master of hiding the truth in plain sight, so when you think you know how it's done, he'll fool you again.'

Adam watched Malachi spin the safe around.

'When you're sitting in the audience, it's hard to work out what he does with the safe, but picking the right card with the knife was more obvious.'

'So how did he do it?'

'Malachi had two packs of cards and someone, perhaps you, told him which card had been chosen.'

Severin laughed. 'That's too complicated for a simple trick.'

Adam frowned at Severin's gentle taunting.

'Perhaps I didn't figure it out, and I'll admit the bullet catch was a good trick.'

'That's because it's not a trick. Malachi really caught the bullet in his teeth.'

Adam waited for Severin to smile, but when he only stared at him, he listened to the banter Malachi exchanged with Lucy.

Malachi offered her a choice of a thousand dollars or his return. He opened the safe to reveal the gold and jewels he'd discovered at the start of the act, and although she wanted the money, the audience shouted for his return.

'Malachi won't give her the money,' Adam said. 'So how am I going to return now that Florence has moved the mirror?'

Severin untied his cloak and let it fall to the floor.

'That depends on whether you're prepared to take your pants off.'

Adam flinched, but Severin smiled while he removed Adam's hat and placed it on his own head. Then he slipped out of his jacket and held it out.

The two men considered each other until, with a burst of understanding, Adam noted the jacket had the same cut as the heckler's jacket. This meant that man was a part of the act and Malachi had picked him only as a last resort.

'You look a bit like me, but not that much.'

'Enough, I hope.' Severin withdrew a dollar from his pocket. 'And if not, this will complete my disguise.'

Two minutes later, Adam had slipped into Severin's clothes, which fitted well, as they should do or else Malachi wouldn't have chosen him, while Severin headed into the shadows.

Now he'd seen how the trick worked,

Adam hoped someone would spot the switch, but as it turned out, nobody did.

Lucy supported the audience's demand that he return, so Malachi closed the safe and turned it while Florence bent over with her back to the audience to brush away imaginary scraps of dirt.

Malachi flung open the door to reveal the safe was empty. Consternation erupted as it looked as if the trick had failed, but when the hoots of derision became deafening, Malachi slammed the door shut and pointed at the audience.

'Who's that sitting beside you?' he demanded. 'It looks as if your young man couldn't bear to be apart from you any longer.'

'It's him!' Lucy screamed with delight, cutting through the hubbub as she stared agog at the smiling Severin, who, unnoticed, had slipped skilfully into Adam's vacated seat.

'I hope he's nice to you,' Malachi said as, with a theatrical gesture, he opened the safe, 'as you turned down a thousand dollars for him.'

The safe's contents made the excited audience erupt from their seats. With raucous applause sounding, Florence shut the safe door while Malachi came to the front of the stage to take the applause.

Then he hurried off the stage, presumably before anyone noticed Lucy's companion had changed, while Florence pushed the safe after him. Once offstage, Malachi stopped to consider Adam.

'You performed well,' he said using a quiet voice that was unlike his booming stage voice, although it was just as authoritative. 'Join us for a celebratory drink.'

'Can I bring Lucy?' Adam asked.

'You can't go out there, for obvious reasons.' Malachi frowned. 'Let Severin bring her, if he returns.'

Malachi cast Florence a sly glance that made her look aloft and, even without checking what was happening in the audience, Adam knew he'd never see Lucy again.

Not that he minded when Florence took his arm and led him to their room backstage.

In the small space that became even more cramped when they'd filled it with the props from their performance, Florence poured him a whiskey. Then she and Malachi removed their make-up while discussing in low tones how well they thought the evening had gone.

Adam sat on a chair that stood beside the safe. He opened the door to find that the gold bars and jewels were now heaped inside, although when he tapped a bar, it returned a hollow sound and he had no doubt the jewels were glass.

'You sure fooled everyone with your tricks,' Adam said when Malachi noted his interest in the fake fortune Lucy had turned down.

'Except you, of course,' Malachi said.

'I saw through some of them, but you fooled me more times than I care to admit.' Adam relaxed when this made Malachi grunt with encouragement.

'And what did you see through?'

'I could tell the heckler who looks like Severin works for you.'

'Why?'

'He was loud and drew attention to himself before you picked him.'

Malachi exchanged a sharp glance with Florence.

'Being noticed by the audience is an essential part of the act.' Malachi sat on a chair opposite him while Florence poured him a drink before she settled down on a chair with Severin's cloak wrapped around her legs. 'But being drunk wasn't part of the act and so whether Derrick still works for me is yet to be decided.'

Adam nodded. 'I understand your irritation. You took a big risk using me.'

'I did, but then again I take a big risk every time I walk on to the stage.' He glanced at Florence. 'We all do.'

'The knife throwing was dangerous, but the bullet catch was a trick.'

Malachi leaned forward and slapped a heavy hand on Adam's knee.

'That was no trick. Men more skilled

than I have died performing that act. I was taught its secret by the true master of the arcane arts, Jubal Jackson. He died on stage before a horrified audience and so I perform the bullet catch in his memory. It's dangerous beyond reason, as I promised.'

His intense gaze made Adam gulp down the rest of his drink.

'I've had to defend myself and I know that every time you fire a gun there's danger, but I also know no man can catch a bullet with his teeth, or at least not without losing his jaw.'

Malachi continued to stare at him until with a snort he leaned back and sipped his drink.

'So tell me: before you came to Bear Creek to seek employment and enjoy a few days of relaxation, why were you sacked?'

Adam flinched. 'How did you know I lost my job?'

Malachi flashed a smile. 'It's a trick.'

Adam considered Malachi and shook his head.

'No, it's an observation. I was with a woman who charges by the hour. I look tired ... ' Adam considered his reflection in a mirror and wondered what other clues his demeanour provided. Then he conceded Malachi's astuteness with a smile. 'I worked for a sharper until his shoddy goods annoyed a customer and he took revenge. The merchant's recovering from a gunshot wound to the butt and I'm out of work.'

'Being a sharper is a dangerous occupation.'

'Less so than being a magician.'

Malachi laughed and raised his glass in salute.

'I like you, but if you're going to work for me, you'll have to learn the difference between reality and misdirection and then understand which wrong direction you've taken.'

Malachi's welcome job offer made Adam smile and, bearing in mind Derrick's performance earlier, he didn't need to ask what kind of job he was being offered.

'Before you perform the bullet catch again, I'll work out how you do it,' Adam said, lost for an appropriate retort.

Malachi opened his mouth wide and then clamped his teeth closed quickly as if catching something.

'You saw how I did it. I snatched the bullet from the air before it could take my jaw away.'

Adam laughed, but Malachi merely looked at him while Florence stood up and slipped between them to head to the door.

'While you two discuss the details, I need to change,' she said throwing the cloak over a spare chair.

She opened the door, but when Malachi raised a hand, she stopped.

'Before you go,' he said, 'I believe Adam would benefit from a demonstration of the reality behind the misdirection.'

She considered for a moment and then nodded and picked her way across the cluttered room. While smiling she slipped behind Adam and placed her hands over his eyes.

'Close your eyes and don't peek,' she whispered in his ear with a giggle. 'It'll spoil the trick.'

Her hands were cool and Adam sensed he would be made to look foolish, but as Florence was involved, he didn't mind.

'And what will you do?' Adam said, turning to Malachi. 'Make me disappear? Make you disappear? Make Florence disappear?'

'As all magicians know, making people disappear is easy,' Malachi said as Florence shuffled her feet to keep her balance on the cluttered floor. 'Bringing them back is harder, and I'm the best.'

Despite his closed eyes, he detected Malachi moving around. Then Florence removed her hands and placed them on his shoulders.

'Open your eyes when I raise my hands,' she said.

She counted down from five and so while smiling Adam waited, and when she lifted her hands, he opened his eyes to find that Florence was standing ten feet away in the doorway. She'd adopted her stage pose with her left leg raised and bent and her right arm thrust high.

'How did . . . ?' Adam murmured. Then he realized Malachi was standing beside him, which meant he and Florence had swapped hands when Florence had taken her hands from his eyes to put them on his shoulders.

He directed a triumphant look at Malachi, but without concern Malachi pointed behind him and so he swirled round. He found himself looking at Florence again, and again she'd adopted her pose, this time while sporting a wide grin.

Adam gulped and turned back to find the doorway was now empty.

'I'm the master of hiding the truth in plain sight,' Malachi said heading to the door. 'So even when you know how the trick works, reality can be more interesting than the misdirection.'

'How?' Adam gasped.

'Do you believe I can catch a bullet with my teeth?'

'No man can do that,' Adam murmured, his shaking delivery conveying he wasn't so certain any more.

'Except the great Malachi Muldoon can.' Malachi clicked his fingers and Florence looked in from the corridor and waved. 'Everything else I do is a trick performed with sleights of hand and mirrors and ringers and . . . and doubles.'

'This is my sister Katherine,' Florence said as she slipped by him to stand with what he now saw was another woman. 'We look a lot more alike than you and Severin, don't you think?'

For the first time that evening, Adam was lost for words.

3

'Surely Ralston Hope wouldn't take a room in Logan Mann's hotel,' Hayward Knight said.

'Ralston's gone to ground and we've looked in the obvious places,' Sheriff Washington said as they walked down the corridor to the end room. 'So now we check out every lead.'

The previous night, Malachi Muldoon's show was all anyone had wanted to talk about, so they hadn't added substance to the rumour of Ralston's return and they'd patrolled the town without success.

That morning they'd heard more rumours, including Ralston having based himself in the last place anybody would expect him to be. But Logan Mann hadn't been downstairs and the receptionist had been vague.

Hayward had looked over the receptionist's shoulder and seen room six was the only occupied room. So they moved on to that room and stood to either side of the door.

'This is Sheriff Washington,' Washington called, while rapping on the door. 'Come out, Ralston. I know you're in there.'

He waited for ten seconds, but silence reigned and so he rapped more forcefully. This time, his action made the door edge open.

Hayward peered through the expanding gap to see a man was standing before the door with his head bowed.

The door creaked making him flinch and look up. When he espied Hayward, he took a backward pace while raising a hand to his forehead.

The man's fair hair and angular features matched Sheriff Washington's description of Ralston Hope, although the scrapes on his cheeks, the matted blood in his hair, and his dishevelled clothing made him look less fearsome than he expected.

Ralston stumbled and fell against the

wall where he stood propped up. So Hayward slipped inside and stood to Ralston's right while Washington stood on his left.

'What happened, Ralston?' Washington asked, his voice neutral and devoid of concern. 'Did someone get to you before you got to them?'

Ralston gave a brief nod and tried to stand unaided, but the effort made him sway. He contemplated the two lawmen with one eye narrowed and the other eye pained and bruised.

'I'll deal with this,' he said.

'You won't.' Washington pointed at the door. 'You deserved that. Now come with me before anyone stirs.'

'And the men who did this?'

'I'll thank them later.'

'I thought so.' Ralston moved on and flopped down into a chair where he sat hunched over and fingering his ribs. 'Leave me alone.'

'You know I can't do that.'

Washington caught Hayward's eye and so Hayward considered the room.

He saw no bags and the only sign Ralston had stayed here was the blankets that had been dragged off the bed, presumably during the struggles that had taken place.

Hayward paced around the room, looking in drawers and throwing open cupboard doors. When he'd searched the obvious places, Washington was still standing over Ralston.

Hayward didn't want to report he'd found nothing incriminating, so he knelt to look under the bed. He saw only dust, but when he felt the heap of blankets, a solid object underneath made him start.

Washington cast him an exasperated glance before grabbing Ralston's shoulder. Ralston tried to bat his hand away, but he failed and Washington drew him to his feet.

While Washington marched Ralston to the door, Hayward shoved the top blanket aside revealing an arm. With mounting trepidation he drew back the other blankets to reveal a woman's body with blood pooled around her.

'Sheriff,' he said with a heavy tone as he confirmed the young woman wouldn't get any older.

Washington stopped and peered over the bed. He grunted with anger and shoved Ralston forward, who in his weakened state went sprawling on the mattress.

Ralston peered at the body before looking at Hayward with an incredulous expression that Hayward didn't think he could have feigned.

'I didn't have anything to do with this,' Ralston murmured. 'I don't even know her name.'

Washington came round the bed to stand beside Hayward.

'That's Lucy Peters from the Rusty Spur,' Washington muttered when he saw her face. 'Sadly nobody told her to refuse your money.'

'This is the first time I've seen her. You have to believe me.'

'I don't believe nothing you say.' Washington dragged Ralston off the bed and on to the door. 'She was at the magic show last night and her escort went up on stage. Did you move in on her then?'

'I'm not saying nothing to a man who won't believe me.'

Ralston dug in a heel, forcing Washington to push him on.

'That's the best news I've heard today.' Washington looked in on Hayward. 'I'll take care of Ralston. You finish up here.'

When Washington and Ralston moved off, Hayward checked the room, but he found nothing of interest and so he knelt beside Lucy.

During his inspection of her clothing, he found no pockets, although he confirmed she had been stabbed in the neck. The wound was ragged suggesting she'd struggled.

Having learnt everything he could, he covered the body with a blanket and went in search of Logan Mann so he could lock the room. Logan wasn't in his office and neither was the reception-ist.

This early in the morning it was unlikely anyone would stumble across the body, so he left the hotel. Five buildings away from the law office, he saw that Ralston's arrest had gathered interest.

The receptionist and another man were engaged in animated conversation on the boardwalk while two of Logan's men, Dale and Gomez, were heading for the office with determined treads. When Hayward reached the office, nobody met Hayward's eye and so he brushed past Dale and Gomez and slipped into the office to find that Logan was talking with Washington.

'Nothing to report other than Lucy was stabbed and she struggled in vain,' Hayward said.

'Poor girl,' Logan said. 'If only I'd had the guts to deal with Ralston the last time, she'd be alive.'

'The last time we had no evidence,' Washington said. He raised a hand when Logan objected. 'We know he did it, but we did the right thing by running him out of town.'

'And this time?'

'That'll depend on whether we can prove his movements last night, including who beat him.'

'I can help you with that.'

Washington considered Logan with his jaw set firm.

'You found him, knocked him about, and dumped him in the room?'

'Sure, and he was alone when I told him to leave town by noon or he'd get the same treatment.'

Washington sighed. 'Provided everyone's honest about their part in last night's activities, we can get what we want.'

'You know that won't happen. Last night was messy. A court won't want to hear about a killer being beaten before killing again.'

Washington sighed. 'What would you have me do?'

'You have until sundown tomorrow to work that out for yourself.' Logan glanced at the door to the jailhouse. 'Then I'll deal with him.'

★ ★ ★

'He can't do my job,' Derrick Fox said, gesturing at Adam.

'Even a drunkard could do what you do,' Malachi said. 'But I don't want him to.'

Derrick sneered at Adam before he vaulted from the stage and slumped down in a chair on the front row, leaving Adam to continue with what would be his only rehearsal.

After accepting Malachi's offer to join his show, he had travelled with them to Carmon. Here, Malachi had a booking and as the auditorium was larger than Bear Creek's, Adam was already nervous.

His role would be the one he had adopted accidentally, except this time he would be a paid ringer. Apparently, in Bear Creek Derrick should have had a saloon girl escort who appeared to others as if she knew him, but who had spent so little time with him she would accept he and Severin were the same person.

40

So before the show started he was to find someone to go with him. Katherine and Florence had found this aspect of his role amusing and they'd whispered to each other while shooting him glances.

Adam hadn't minded their attention as, since he'd been hired, they had preferred their own company.

He could now see they weren't as alike as he'd first thought. Katherine was the older sister and she could be mistaken for Florence only when they were made-up and dressed identically.

Malachi and Derrick also kept their own company, with Malachi appearing deep in thought and Derrick being surly. Only Severin was friendly and his amiable demeanour meant Adam had forgiven him for leaving with Lucy.

When Adam had picked a seat ten chairs away from Derrick, Florence sat beside him in her guise as his escort.

'Aren't you needed on stage?' Adam asked.

'We're doing the act we did in Bear

Creek, so I'm on stage only at the start and at the end.' She laughed when Adam looked at her with surprise. 'You were watching Katherine for most of the show, while I stayed out of sight moving the fake fortune.'

Adam sighed. 'You're good at what you do. How long have you worked for Malachi?'

'We used to work for Jubal Jackson, the magician who taught Malachi the bullet catch. Three years ago, when Jubal died, we formed a new act with Malachi.'

Adam nodded and settled down to see how Malachi performed his tricks. But the rehearsal explained nothing as Malachi merely walked through the acts while noting the size of the stage and deciding where he and Katherine would stand.

Only when he came to Derrick's new role did he go into detail. Derrick would be the impartial audience member who verified the gun was loaded before being amazed when Malachi caught the bullet.

Derrick had to speak every line from his script to Malachi's satisfaction. So Derrick showed his irritation with a monotone delivery and, when Malachi deemed his part complete, he stormed off the stage.

Malachi watched him leave while shaking his head. So, reckoning his role could soon become permanent and larger, Adam concentrated on performing his section properly.

Malachi told him to adopt the role of a reluctant audience member, who had only stood up to bat dust off his seat and who needed encouragement to go up on stage.

'I'm not volunteering,' Adam said with a faltering voice while pointing at his chair. 'My seat's dirty.'

Katherine and Florence applauded, and Malachi smiled.

'I like that,' Malachi said. 'That should get a laugh.'

Then he and Malachi rehearsed his reluctant man act before Adam went up on stage where he followed Malachi's instructions meekly. He spoke only when he was asked questions while presenting the air of a man who was too insignificant to be a part of the act.

When they'd finished the rehearsal, Malachi took Adam aside.

'You were believable and confident,' he said.

'I feel confident now.' Adam considered the safe. 'But what would you do if the escort wants the money?'

'They never do. I'm a magician. They always pick the card I want them to pick.' Malachi winked and lowered his voice. 'But if Derrick can't complete his part, could you do that, too?'

'I heard his lines, so I reckon I can.'

Malachi patted his back as they left the stage.

'I'd prefer to have two ringers, so I hope it won't come to that.' He pointed at the door. 'Now run along, it's show time in an hour and you need an escort. Make sure she's fetching. That always works well.'

Florence heard the last order and she

muttered under her breath before turning on her heels, making Malachi smile. So with the intriguing possibility she was unhappy because he had to find a saloon girl, Adam headed to the Tenderfoot saloon beside the music hall.

Within a minute of entering the saloon room, three women approached him. Figuring his task would be easy, he rebuffed them to give him time to work out which one would provide the best reaction.

He sat at the bar with the relaxed demeanour of a man intent on entertainment until with a wince he noted Derrick was sitting at the opposite end of the bar. He nodded to him and even though Derrick didn't respond, he joined him.

'Malachi told me he prefers having two ringers,' Adam said. 'So you have nothing to fear.'

'Malachi's confiding in you now, is he?' Derrick said sourly. He leaned over his drained whiskey glass. 'I've been with him for years and he never consults me on nothing.'

Adam ordered two drinks to give him time to think of a way to find out what was troubling Derrick.

'I'm pleased Malachi employed me,' he said when he had a full glass. 'In my previous job I nearly got shot up. So I welcome working for Malachi where all I have to do is move equipment and sit in the audience with a saloon girl waiting to say a few lines.'

Derrick gulped his liquor in a determined manner suggesting that when the show started, he'd be as inebriated as he had been in Bear Creek.

'You'll tire of it, but that won't matter because you won't last for long.' Derrick knocked back the rest of his drink.

'Is that a threat?' Adam said, squaring up to him.

Derrick glanced at him from the corner of his eye and laughed.

'No. I feel sorry for you. You don't

know nothing and now it's too late.' He hunched over the bar, showing he didn't want to continue with this conversation.

'Why is it too late?' Adam persisted.

Derrick ignored him and ordered another whiskey, this time asking the bartender to leave the bottle. With a snort of derision, Adam pushed his own untouched drink along the bar so it nudged against Derrick's arm.

He walked away and his expression must have betrayed his irritation as nobody approached him. He didn't calm down until he stood outside on the boardwalk drinking in the cool evening air.

Carmon had three other saloons. He chose the Wild Horse across the main drag, but he'd taken a single step on to the hardpan when footfalls sounded behind him and whiskey laden breath washed over him.

'Perhaps it's not too late to stop Malachi,' Derrick said.

'I'm not . . . ' Adam trailed off when steel poked into his back.

He stopped and looked along the road. With sundown imminent, dozens of people were about, but none of them paid him any attention.

'Walk on and act friendly,' Derrick said, with an encouraging poke in the back.

As requested, Adam started walking away from the music hall.

'As we're being friendly, why are you doing this?' Adam said.

'I'm saving your life.'

'How?' Adam walked on for ten paces, but when Derrick didn't respond, he persisted. 'I can see you have a problem with Malachi, but I don't know what — '

'Be quiet,' Derrick snapped. With a glance around, he directed him to head to the side of a stable.

Adam said nothing, but when they moved away from the main drag into the shadows, concern made his heart thud. So he looked around for an opportunity to fight back before it was too late.

When they reached the far corner of

the stable, the evening sounds from the road receded. As only scrub land was beyond, Adam turned sharply and threw up a hand aiming to slap Derrick's gun aside.

He moved quickly enough to knock Derrick's gun arm against the stable wall, but Derrick reacted with a fierce uppercut that crunched Adam's teeth together. Adam backed away while shaking his head to regain his senses.

Before he could shake off the blow, Derrick thudded a short-armed jab into his stomach that made him fold over. Then a firm blow on the back made him stumble into the stable wall face first.

Derrick grabbed the back of his jacket and hammered his forehead against the wall, and then again, making the wall rattle so loudly Adam thought he would break through.

After the last blow, Derrick held him firmly with one arm held up his back and with his face mashed against the wood.

'I'm no threat to you,' Adam murmured.

'But you're a threat to yourself. One day you'll thank me for this.'

With a flick of the wrist, Derrick turned his gun around. Adam was opening his mouth to retort when a heavy blow hammered against the back of his head.

Unable to control his body, he slid down to his knees and on to his chest. He locked his gaze on a stone lying before him and willed himself to keep his eyes open, but darkness still overcame him.

4

'Logan Mann's here,' Hayward Knight said, peering out of the window.

Washington joined him at the window to watch Logan, along with his two most troublesome hired men Dale and Gomez, walk towards the law office. Like yesterday they had determined strides.

Since yesterday Hayward and Washington had failed to trace Lucy's movements in the hours before she'd died and they were no nearer to proving, or disproving, that Ralston Hope had killed her. But when Logan came in, he had other matters on his mind.

'Four years ago Ralston Hope killed my sister Mary by slashing her throat,' he said, talking softly. 'There were no witnesses and Ralston wouldn't talk. Back then, I said we should string him up and you said we should run him out of town. You won. This time, I'll deal with him.'

Hayward stood at Washington's shoulder, expecting he'd have to back him up during a difficult confrontation, but to his surprise Washington hunched his shoulders and stared at the floor in a resigned way.

'All right,' he said, his voice small.

'You can't,' Hayward spluttered as Logan smirked.

Washington turned to him. 'You know this is the only way. Fetch the key to Ralston's cell.'

Through the window Hayward considered Dale and Gomez on the boardwalk awaiting the outcome of this debate. They had the subdued postures of men who knew what they'd have to do and who didn't relish the prospect.

'This is wrong. We don't know yet that Ralston killed Lucy.' He waved his hands as he struggled to find the words to appease men who had already made up their minds. 'I'm not sure he'd even seen her before. We have to investigate this properly.'

'We did that four years ago. Except

Ralston's still alive to kill. I'm not taking that chance again.'

Washington moved on to get the key, forcing Hayward to take a sideways step to block his way.

'Lucy was last seen leaving the magic show with a man. He could have killed her. In fact, dozens of people at the show could have done it.'

As Logan snorted at this unlikely possibility, Washington shook his head, although he still struggled to meet his eye.

'Move aside.'

Hayward stood his ground, which made Dale and Gomez pick up on the situation. As they slipped inside, with a weary nod Hayward accepted he had no choice and he held out a hand for the key.

'I don't reckon I can stomach a necktie party,' he said with a sigh. 'But perhaps you're right and it's time I learnt about the reality of justice.'

His change of heart made Washington consider him. Then he gave a brief nod and so Hayward took the key and headed into the adjoining jailhouse.

In his cell Ralston was sitting hunched over on his cot staring at the floor. Ralston would have heard the debate about his fate and so Hayward moved cautiously. He rattled the key against a bar before opening the cell door.

He kept his hand beside his holster while he waited for Ralston to acknowledge him, which he did slowly while rubbing his bruised cheek.

'I didn't kill Lucy,' Ralston said. 'This is wrong.'

'Whether you did it or not, it won't make no difference,' Hayward said. 'This is happening because you killed Mary Mann.'

Ralston sighed. Then he got to his feet where he stretched and winced.

'I could never hurt Mary. I loved her. And I had nothing to do with Lucy's death either. So every moment you waste on me gives her killer another moment to get away.'

'The dead woman was in your room. That means you're the best place to start to find the killer.'

Hayward beckoned and Ralston moved forward, but he stopped beside Hayward and considered him, his hunched shoulders suggesting he was debating whether to reveal more.

'Forget me. Head east and follow the real killer.'

'Which one? Lucy's killer or Mary's killer?'

'I believe they're the same.' This time Hayward didn't reply, encouraging Ralston to fill the silence and sure enough, with a heavy sigh Ralston continued. 'Four years ago I took Mary to a magic show. The magician said he'd make someone from the audience disappear and I got called up on stage.'

'Did you disappear?'

'It was a trick. When I went backstage, someone who looked like me sat beside Mary. Afterwards, she left with him. I followed them and found her. She'd been stabbed. When Logan found me I had blood on my hands. It looked bad. Logan didn't believe I'd only found her body, but your boss needed more proof.'

Hayward glanced through the jailhouse window. In the law office Logan and Washington were talking, giving him time to ask more questions.

'He's an astute man, but I'm surprised he hasn't mentioned the obvious link between Lucy's death and Mary's.'

'He didn't believe my story. He said everyone blames strangers. Either way, it was a different magic show. Jubal Jackson ran the show, not Malachi Muldoon.'

'The name means nothing to me.'

'Nor me, except last month I was in Monotony and everyone was talking about a woman being attacked. It was rumoured that someone from a magic show did it. I followed the show and risked heading into Bear Creek to check it out.'

'Different show and a different

magician, but the same story,' Hayward mused.

Washington and Logan had now stopped talking and they were looking into the jailhouse, clearly wondering why he was taking so long, so Hayward ushered Ralston away from his cell and into the law office.

'I hope his last words were good ones,' Washington said, considering Hayward. 'Everything else he's ever told me has been lies.'

Hayward took the hint that he should treat Ralston's tale with scepticism. He stood aside, but he resolved not to stop thinking about what he'd been told.

Washington gestured for Ralston to hold out his hands. He secured his wrists using a tightly knotted rope and with a long sigh, he passed the other end to Logan, suggesting he wasn't as comfortable with this turn of events as he'd claimed.

Then, with control having been passed on, Logan organized his men. He ordered Dale to walk behind

Ralston while he handed the rope to Gomez.

He didn't explain their plan and the men moved with downbeat demeanours. Ralston was led outside with the lawmen following on behind.

While he'd been in the jailhouse, an open wagon had been drawn up and between it and the law office, two lines of men showed Ralston the way.

For his part Ralston looked beyond his guards, presumably hoping he would attract attention from sympathetic people, but it was early evening and only Logan's men were outside.

With his head held high, Ralston moved on to the wagon, although as his hands were tied Gomez had to help him on to the back. He sat against the side while two men sat opposite, two men sat on either side, and Gomez sat at the back.

Logan joined Dale on the seat and, when Dale trundled the wagon off at a steady pace, the lawmen headed to their horses. Washington moved slowly and Hayward got the impression he wanted to speak with him, so he tried to catch his eye, but whatever was troubling him, he didn't pass it on.

When they'd mounted up, they followed the wagon and at a sombre pace they headed out of town.

The reason for the steady pace soon became clear, as Logan was taking Ralston only to an abandoned stable a mile out of town. The wooden walls were rotten and listing, but the ramshackle building felt appropriate for the occasion even before Washington leaned from the saddle and explained.

'Logan found Mary's body here,' he said. 'Nobody's used the place since.'

With Washington appearing ready to talk, Hayward chose his next words carefully.

'Are you sure Ralston killed Mary?'

'No.'

'Then why are we letting this happen?'

Washington watched the wagon slow as it slipped through the doorway and drew to a halt.

'Because the deal I made with

Ralston in return for his release is that he'd never come back.'

'But if we let this happen, how can we keep the peace?'

'If we stop this, how can we keep it?'

Washington moved his horse on to stand beside the doorway and when Hayward joined him, he saw that Dale had stopped the wagon beneath a beam that stretched across the stable. Ralston was showing admirable forbearance and he looked through the door, perhaps enjoying his last sight of the outside world.

Gomez dragged Ralston to his feet beneath the beam and then prepared a noose. When Ralston planted his feet wide apart to keep his balance, Hayward considered his options, but nobody had followed them out of town and he saw no possibility of mercy from Logan as he stood before the wagon directing operations.

Once Gomez had made the noose, he threw it over the beam and dragged it down to head height on the wagon. Gomez hurried on to secure the rope, leaving nobody standing between Ralston and Logan.

'You're a low-down snake and your sister hated you,' Ralston said glaring at Logan.

'Be quiet,' Logan said. 'You don't deserve no last words.'

'But you deserve to hear them. I cared for Mary and we planned to leave town and start a new life together, except you couldn't accept that. I never hurt her. Severin O'Hara from the magic show killed her.'

Logan glared at Ralston making Ralston appear to remember he wasn't giving Logan the satisfaction of seeing him in distress, and he stood tall.

For the next two minutes Logan and Ralston faced each other as Gomez wrapped the noose around Ralston's neck and the other preparations were completed. Dale stayed on the seat while the rest of Logan's men lined up before the doorway to witness Ralston's demise.

With everyone having their backs to

him, Hayward resolved that the moment Logan ordered Dale to move on, confirming beyond all doubt he'd go through with this, he would step in. He doubted he'd be successful and he could think of no plan that would improve his chances.

But when Logan looked past Ralston to check Dale was in position, Sheriff Washington edged forward, forcing the two men to step aside.

'I want to hear more about this Severin O'Hara,' he said levelly. 'This goes no further until I've heard Ralston's full tale.'

Hayward breathed a sigh of relief, realizing his boss had done what he'd planned to do by letting this situation play out and see what developed before he stepped in. Clearly Ralston had never volunteered a name before, but as he moved forward to join his boss, Logan glared at Washington.

'You agreed I'd get justice.'

'And you will. When Ralston told me his tale before, he always kept something back, but I reckon you've got him into the right frame of mind to tell us everything now.'

'You can't take his word about anything,' Logan spluttered. 'And what about Lucy Peters?'

'She deserves real justice, too, and I don't reckon Ralston killed her. When I found him, he could barely stand, never mind kill someone.' Washington turned to Ralston. 'So talk, Ralston, or I'll leave you with Logan.'

For long moments the men stood in silence, with everyone looking to Logan for his reaction. Logan delivered his verdict when he pointed at Dale.

'I already know the truth and we're hanging Ralston tonight,' he shouted. He jerked the hand down. 'Ride!'

5

Adam stared into the darkness, feeling confused until he saw the stars. This let him orient himself and work out he was lying on his back behind the stable.

It had been lighter when Derrick had attacked him, so time had passed. With a hand to his brow, he gingerly got to his knees.

The movement made his head pound and so he stared at the ground gulping down a nauseous feeling. When the urge to vomit faded, he got to his feet, setting off another round of sickness, but this time he kept moving and worked his way around the stable wall.

When he reached the next corner he paused for breath. The throbbing in his head had reduced to a dull ache while the nausea had passed, so while leaning against the wall, he considered the main drag.

Boisterous noise came from the two nearest saloons, but few people were outside. He failed to locate a clock, but he judged it was mid-evening.

That meant Malachi's show would be underway and he might already have missed his part. This failing would probably lose him his job and when Derrick, presumably, stepped in to save the situation it'd make him popular again with Malachi.

Adam set off for the music hall at a slow pace, pausing to put a hand to the wall every five paces. Despite his growing strength and his less befuddled senses, he struggled to work out why Derrick had knocked him out to improve his prospects when those prospects weren't at risk if he stayed sober.

Then he recalled the cryptic things Derrick had said about stopping Malachi and he peered at the music hall. A sense of foreboding made him gulp.

He didn't know what had gone on between the people in Malachi's show before he'd met them, but clearly there was bad blood. Then there was the death of Jubal Jackson, the previous man to perform the bullet catch.

Nobody had suggested this wasn't an accident, but Derrick's recent behaviour made Adam wonder if it wasn't.

He hurried across the road, his belief that he'd deduced the situation growing with every pace. When he reached the boardwalk, applause was coming from within the building and as the bullet catch was done in silence, that meant he still had time to avert disaster.

Two guards were at the door and they closed ranks to bar his way.

'The show's started,' one man said.

'And the hall's full,' the other man said as they both folded their arms.

'There has to be room for one more,' Adam said. 'I'm part of the show.'

'Then you're on the wrong side of this door,' the first man said with the inevitable logic of someone who enjoyed being awkward. 'And that's where you're staying.'

Adam considered both men, noting their hulking forms and firm jaws.

'All right,' he said, figuring he'd only waste time trying to talk them round. He cast his mind back and recalled the back door would be open during the performance to let in cool air. 'I'll get in the back way.'

He stayed until the confident expressions on both men's faces flickered. Then he turned away.

Both men moved to block his way, but Adam had anticipated that action and he neatly turned back, ducked under one man's flailing arm, and reached the doorway. The sudden movement made his head thud and he stumbled as he moved on, but that saved him when the second man lunged at him from behind and his arms merely brushed across his back.

He turned his stumble into a run and with faltering paces he headed across the foyer to the door to the auditorium. Nobody was patrolling this door and he reached it three paces ahead of his pursuers, but the gap closed when he wasted valuable seconds throwing open the door.

He slipped around the door and swung it into the face of the closest man. Then, while moving on, he took stock of the situation.

Thankfully, the show hadn't reached his part yet and, even more thankfully, Malachi had yet to perform the bullet catch. He was preparing the act though as the masked Severin was on stage while Katherine was rooting around for the brand.

The scene appeared the same as it had done the first time he'd seen the act, but a woman and not Derrick was standing beside Katherine having come on stage to verify the gun was loaded. As Derrick had no excuse for not being there, he probably planned to sabotage the performance, possibly fatally.

Adam peered around the room, searching for Derrick. He'd examined only two rows when one of his pursuers slammed into his back and pushed him on to press him against the wall, while the second man stood between him and the stage.

'All these good people paid,' his assailant muttered in his ear. 'You didn't.'

'I'll pay,' Adam gasped, struggling to form the words with the man's weight trapping him against the wall.

'No room available.' The man gathered a firm grip of his arm and turned him to the door. 'Except for outside.'

'Malachi,' Adam called, but as he was still gaining his breath, his voice was no louder than his normal speaking voice and it didn't cut through the audience's contented murmuring.

He struggled, but the pressure on his back was relentless and, with a stumbling gait, the guard moved him on to the door.

'As I don't want my good friend Penelope to regret coming up on stage, I need complete silence,' Malachi announced from the stage. He lowered his tone. 'But in case I don't defy death, my killer is wearing a mask to ensure his identity will never become known.'

As had happened before, silence descended on the room, and so, accepting this gave him his only chance, Adam went limp to let his captor move him to the door quickly.

The second man hurried on, and when he pushed the door open, the brightness from outside illuminated the three men. Adam took a half-step to place both feet together and then with his back braced against the guard's chest, he raised his feet and planted them against the door jamb.

He pushed backwards, but the guard stood solidly and his efforts only arched his back. His failure to dislodge his captor didn't concern Adam as he took a deep breath and shouted.

'Malachi, don't try to catch the bullet!' he roared.

As people on the back rows turned to the commotion, the second guard grabbed Adam's legs and dragged them away from the door, but that only gave

Adam a target to kick. With a wild sweep of his right leg Adam caught the man a glancing blow to his chin that made him jerk backward and release his legs.

Adam's feet crashed back down on the floor heavily pulling his captor forward and so Adam encouraged the motion by bending double. His captor pressed down on his back and in a tangle of limbs the two men went down.

Then Adam was punched and manhandled from several directions. He didn't mind if the guards took out their irritation on him as long as he got Malachi's attention and so he sought to crawl away.

To his surprise, he dragged himself clear of the tussle. He glanced over his shoulder to see that several audience members had ploughed into the fray to subdue it without knowing who was in the right or wrong.

The guards were struggling to extricate themselves from the mass of people and so Adam broke into a run. Within a few paces he saw the chaos at the back of the room had gathered the audience's attention and everyone was gesturing and encouraging the participants to desist.

Better still, on the stage Malachi had his hands on his hips while Katherine and the masked Severin stood together waiting for order to be restored. In twenty long paces, Adam reached the stage and rolled on to it to stand before Malachi.

'What's the reason for this rude intrusion?' Malachi demanded, showing no sign he recognized him, presumably to maintain the illusion they hadn't met before.

Adam raised a cautionary hand and looked at the audience, seeking out Derrick. He could see only irritated people who were either beckoning him to get off the stage or straining their necks to watch the fight that was gathering its own momentum.

He finished his consideration of the

room facing Malachi. Even though his boss wasn't showing he knew him, he was glaring with a narrowed-eyed expression that said unless his reason was a good one, his employment had ended.

Adam took a deep breath, figuring he'd already gone too far and he couldn't worry about revealing what he knew of Malachi's secrets.

'Derrick attacked me,' he said rubbing the back of his head and wincing. 'I reckon he plans to kill you.'

Malachi's gaze darted to the audience with a tell-tale sign he thought this possible.

'We argued,' he said, speaking quietly so only Adam could hear. 'But that's not a reason to kill me, surely?'

Adam couldn't think of an appropriate reply other than to look again for Derrick. The guards had gathered reinforcements and were ending the fight by throwing everyone that had got involved through the door, but their actions combined with the awkward situation on stage was spreading unrest through the rest of the audience.

'Get on with the show,' someone shouted above the general hubbub and that encouraged other people to repeat the complaint.

'Only you can know whether he's that annoyed with you,' Adam said.

Adam looked at Katherine for support and when Katherine shrugged, Malachi turned to Severin, who stood impassively, and that made him consider the gun sitting on the silver tray.

'Derrick would know how to kill me secretly,' he said.

As the audience's chanting grew louder with everyone urging them to carry on with the performance, Katherine followed Malachi's gaze to the gun.

'Derrick could have swapped the bullet,' she murmured.

The debate encouraged Penelope, the audience member who had checked the gun, to step forward.

'I saw the bullet, and everything's safe,' she declared.

'And everything is safe,' Malachi said, speaking loudly to address her and the audience as he regained his authority. 'But danger stalks my every move and so I must be sure of everything.'

Malachi faced the audience, but his attempt to dismiss the confusion as being theatrics failed when the chanting grew abusive. Worse, the door at the back opened to reveal the fight was raging outside and this made more people decide they'd get more entertainment from those events than from the stage.

As Malachi called for calm, Penelope picked up the gun and punched out the bullet. She deposited it on the tray with a clatter.

'There's no problem,' she declared. 'This is a real bullet. So are you going to catch it, or not?'

'Not,' Malachi said with a gulp. 'Or at least not tonight.'

6

With mounting horror Hayward watched Dale raise the reins while, in a co-ordinated move, Logan's men closed ranks before Washington, who jumped down from his horse to confront them.

Within moments the men surrounded Hayward, keeping him away from the stable, while in the building the wagon rolled forward forcing Ralston to walk along it to the back.

Washington pushed one man aside, which encouraged the other men to manhandle him and so, with a sideways step the sheriff fought his way clear. He turned to Hayward while fishing in his pocket for a knife, which he tossed to him.

Hayward caught the knife and rode on, heedless of the men blocking his path to the stable and so forcing them to leap aside to avoid being trampled.

When he reached the doorway, he drew up and twisted out of the saddle.

He leapt on to the back of the wagon, landing beside Ralston as he shuffled along the base, his boots now inches away from the edge. With only moments to act before Ralston dropped, Hayward put the knife to the taut rope at the back of Ralston's head.

He scythed upwards trying to sever the rope with one slash. The knife bit deeply, but it caught in the rope and Hayward wasted valuable moments tearing it away.

By the time he was ready to try again, only Ralston's heels catching on the back kept him on the wagon. So Hayward had to grip the rope above the cut to avoid falling off the end of the wagon.

He scythed again, putting weight down on a foot that landed on air. Then he fell.

For a terrible moment he thought he'd left Ralston dangling, but then the two men hit the ground heavily on their sides facing each other. Ralston wasted no time before he presented Hayward with his bound hands.

Shadows were spreading over them as Logan's men moved in and so Hayward slipped the knife between Ralston's wrists and with a rapid sawing motion he cut through the rope. The moment the bonds fell away Ralston leapt to his feet, a previously bound fist rising to punch the nearest man.

Hayward followed him, gaining his feet so quickly he stumbled towards Logan's men who were moving in to subdue Ralston. He dragged Gomez away from the tight circle that surrounded their target.

Then he moved to barge the next man aside, but before he could lay a hand on him a gunshot sounded making everyone flinch. All eyes turned to Sheriff Washington who stood with his gun thrust high.

'Back away from him or the next shot will be lower,' he said.

'You're making a big mistake defying me again,' Logan said.

'You should be grateful I'm not arresting you.'

With Logan glowering at him, Washington signified for Hayward to take custody of Ralston. So with the other man not resisting, he shoved them aside to reach Ralston, who had been trying to wrestle Dale to the ground.

The two men extricated themselves leaving Ralston to look at the swinging rope and breathe a sigh of relief. Then he joined Hayward, although he did look beyond the stable as he perhaps contemplated making a bolt for freedom.

'Obliged,' he said.

'Co-operate and you might avoid that noose permanently,' Hayward said.

'You've helped explain some of what happened here four years ago,' Washington said, addressing everybody. 'When we've explained the rest, we'll all rest easy.'

'I'll never rest easy while Ralston lives,' Logan shouted. His face reddened. Then he scrambled for his gun.

Several men were standing between him and Logan and so Hayward moved to push Ralston aside, but Ralston hadn't been Logan's target.

A gunshot rattled and Washington cried out. Through the throng of people Hayward saw the sheriff's gun drop from his hand. Then he followed the gun and fell.

With Logan and his men standing in shocked silence, Ralston bolted. He barged between two men to reach free space and ran for Washington's horse.

Nobody tried to stop him with even Logan watching the wounded lawman. Hayward ran to Washington's side, but before he reached him he saw the copious blood that coated his chest.

With Logan showing no inclination to shoot again, Hayward kept his gun on him and knelt. He shook Washington's shoulder, but the sheriff's head lolled and his eyes were blank and unseeing.

With anger making his heart race, he looked up at Logan.

'This is what happens when men take the law into their own hands,' he spat. 'You'll all pay for this.'

Logan jerked his gun hand up, forcing Hayward to aim at him, although he then saw Logan was aiming over his head.

'Not you,' Logan said, his tone low. 'I want Ralston.'

Logan fired two rapid shots, making Hayward look over his shoulder, but the gunshots had been wild. Ralston had already mounted up and, without a backwards glance, he galloped off.

Hayward got to his feet and backed away while watching everyone.

'No more shooting,' Hayward said. 'I'll get Ralston. You've done enough damage already.'

Logan ignored him and he took careful aim at the fleeing man, but Hayward still ran for his horse and by the time he'd mounted up, Ralston was two hundred yards on and heading away from town.

Logan blasted out a sustained volley

of gunfire into the night, but as Hayward began his pursuit, Logan's wild gunfire petered out.

When Hayward had matched Ralston's speed, he looked over his shoulder. Logan had gathered his men. Then, in a purposeful manner, they clambered into the wagon and set off for town suggesting that despite his order, they'd follow soon.

Hayward cast a last look at the dead sheriff. Then he turned his attention to the chase.

He fell in behind Ralston and although the chance of freedom lay ahead, the battered rider rode stiffly, letting Hayward gain on him.

'You've got nowhere to run,' Hayward shouted over the pounding hoofs. 'Stop now!'

Ralston glanced at Hayward and then over his shoulder. Hayward looked back to confirm Logan and his men had disappeared from view.

'I'm free,' Ralston shouted. 'I'm not getting caught by nobody.'

Hayward nodded, but he kept galloping. They were heading east and even though the evening darkness was deepening, hilly ground where Ralston might find somewhere to hole up was still five miles away.

Judging that Ralston would have to rest his horse soon, Hayward slipped in beside him and matched his speed.

'Logan won't harm you, but I will.'

Hayward drew his gun. They were galloping and so even from five yards away he couldn't be sure of hitting him the first time, but he levelled the gun on Ralston's chest.

For several long strides Ralston gripped the reins tightly, looking as if he'd try an evasive manoeuvre, but then with a resigned shrug of the shoulders he drew back. When they'd both halted, the two riders faced each other.

Ralston sat tall in the saddle and fingered his ribs and his back while wincing as he located sore spots.

'What now, then?' Ralston asked.

Hayward looked back towards town

and then to the east. He rubbed his jaw before offering Ralston a thin smile.

'I'll make Logan pay for what he did,' he said. 'But first, I guess I should check out your story, which means we follow the magic show and find Severin.'

* * *

'It's a disaster,' Walcott Quinn, the music hall owner, said for the third time in as many minutes while pacing his small office. 'A disaster.'

'A disaster would be someone being brutally murdered,' Malachi said with a smile that Walcott didn't return. 'That didn't happen.'

'It didn't, but it could have done. A riot raged outside, your act was forced off the stage, and I had to refund everyone.'

'That was generous of you,' Malachi said with a strained tone that acknowledged that no matter what he said, Walcott would berate him.

The so-called riot had been the aggrieved people taking out their anger on the guards who had waylaid Adam, while the act had been curtailed when the audience hadn't liked Malachi's decision not to risk performing the bullet catch. And Adam hadn't seen anybody getting a refund as the audience had dispersed quickly.

These facts didn't concern Walcott as he glared at Malachi while gesturing angrily to punctuate each of his points.

'I have friends everywhere. Your name will be dirt. You'll never work again.'

Malachi's eyes glazed and he provided a fixed frown that the rest of his people had already adopted while they waited for Walcott's tirade to run out of steam. Irritatingly, it took a while and when Walcott finally sent them to their room, after ordering them to leave his premises within the hour, Malachi had failed to placate him.

'So I guess that means we won't get paid,' Severin said.

The sisters snorted laughs, but Malachi said nothing until they reached their room and then he closed the door and stood before it.

'Has anyone seen Derrick?' he asked. When everyone shook their heads, he looked at Adam.

'I haven't seen him since he knocked me out behind the stable.' Adam fingered the bump on his head.

'I'm grateful you shook off the effects of his assault in time.' Malachi considered him. 'So how would you feel if in return I offered you the chance to get more glimpses into our secrets?'

'Sore,' Adam said casually, although Malachi's eager expression suggested his answer was as important to him as Derrick's duplicity. 'But I guess it depends on whether I still have a job.'

'You saved my life. You can stay with us for as long as you wish.'

'That's good, but I was asking whether any of us have a job?'

Malachi laughed for the first time since they'd left the stage in disgrace.

'Don't despair, my young friend. We've faced worse times than this. Yet despite the setbacks, we still have our most exciting ever booking in Prudence to look forward to. And it's for two nights.'

Adam nodded, but Severin spoke up using a low tone.

'Adam has a point,' he said. 'Walcott will have contacts and he looked angry enough to want to ruin our booking in Prudence.'

'I've performed in Prudence for years and we'll be amongst friends. If anyone hears about tonight, the events will add a layer of mystery and excitement: a fight, a lively audience, and an act that was so dangerous it had to be abandoned. People will pay to see that!'

Severin glanced at Adam, who smiled at the way Malachi was turning the unfortunate situation to their advantage. Although Katherine and Florence grinned, Severin continued with a sombre tone.

'And if we see Derrick?'

Malachi winked. 'We'll hire him again to add an air of danger to the performance.'

Severin took the opportunity to lighten up and he nodded, but with the meeting looking as if it'd end, Florence spoke up.

'Severin's right to be worried,' she said sombrely, Severin's pessimism seemingly now affecting her. 'That was the worst night I've had on stage since Jubal's unfortunate accident. If people suspect the bullet catch is a trick, it'll ruin the performance whether Walcott tries to destroy us or not.'

Malachi gave a brief nod before embarking on a steady walk back and forth while holding a hand to his head in a theatrical gesture of him thinking. Then he stopped and pointed at Adam.

'When people think they know how a trick is performed, what do we do?'

All eyes turned to Adam and so he thought back to his first meeting with

Malachi in another back room like this one.

'You always hide the truth in plain sight,' he said. 'So perform the trick in a different way and show them that what they thought you were doing was in fact not what you were doing.'

He shrugged at his badly worded explanation, but it made Malachi click his fingers.

'During your short time with me you've learnt plenty. If there's a chance that people will see through me, Prudence will be the place for me to risk everything and go beyond the bullet catch to astonish everyone with my courage.'

The other three people opened their mouths in surprise and looked at each other for their reactions. So with nobody asking for an explanation, Adam raised a hand.

'What does that entail?'

'The bullet catch is the most dangerous act that has ever been performed. I intend to better it.' Malachi walked across the room and slapped both hands on

Adam's shoulders to hold his attention as he stared into his eyes. 'In Prudence, we will perform the world's first ever bullet catch showdown!'

7

'Did you ask about Severin O'Hara from Malachi's magic show?' the newcomer Patrick said.

'Sure,' Hayward said. He got off his barstool while Ralston leaned back to appraise Patrick.

'Then come with me.'

Patrick turned to the door and so Hayward and Ralston followed.

It was late afternoon and they'd been in Carmon since noon. Hayward had accepted that Ralston wanted to get to the truth and after securing a promise from him not to run, they had split up to try their different approaches.

When they'd met up and compared notes, they'd both received only guarded answers about Malachi's show. All they had learnt was that the show had left this morning for Prudence, although the people who had told them this had smiled knowingly as if the departure had been an interesting one.

With it now looking as if they'd soon learn more, both men walked down the boardwalk quickly, but Patrick offered no further information. When they approached a hotel where few people were about and Patrick directed them to the back of the hotel, Ralston became agitated.

'Who are you taking us to?' he asked.

Patrick didn't stop and he didn't speak until he reached the far corner of the hotel away from the main drag.

'I'll get paid whether you come with me or not,' he called over his shoulder.

Patrick walked around the corner leaving Ralston and Hayward looking at each other.

'This situation is odd,' Ralston said. 'But we won't learn nothing by waiting here.'

Hayward gave a reluctant nod and so they headed around the corner to find Patrick was leaning against the wall beside a short florid-faced man.

'What's your interest in Malachi's show?' this man asked, after identifying himself as Walcott Quinn, the music hall owner.

'Malachi is a friend,' Hayward said.

His badge was in his pocket as he reckoned that showing it in another town wouldn't help him. He also figured the truth wouldn't get him answers from a man who had probably employed Malachi.

Walcott sneered. 'You're a rare breed, but at least you can answer the questions he left in his wake.'

'I was hoping you'd . . . ' Hayward trailed off when Walcott's gaze flicked past his shoulder.

He turned to find four rough-clad men were striding towards them. Their stern postures made Hayward move off.

He'd taken a single step when Logan Mann along with Dale and Gomez appeared at the other corner. Hayward exchanged an aggrieved glance with Ralston before he barged Walcott aside using a back-handed swipe.

Ralston hurried on and confronted two men from the first group. He delivered quick, wild blows while always moving on.

Hayward reckoned Ralston had the right idea that they should extricate themselves from this situation quickly and so he squared up to his next opponent with his fists raised while advancing determinedly. When the man threw a punch at his head, Hayward ducked beneath it and ran on doubled over.

Even though he had a clear path ahead, Hayward charged one of Ralston's assailants from behind. He caught him with a low shoulder in the back and shoved him on until he slammed into the wall.

By then the other men were moving in to take the place of the ones they'd defeated, so Ralston bundled his second opponent aside. Then they turned on their heels and ran.

Hayward grabbed the corner of the hotel and swung round, the momentum launching him on his way. With Ralston at his heels he pounded along and they covered half the distance to the next corner in seconds.

A gunshot blasted kicking dust from the wall ahead of him.

'The next shot will take you down,' Logan shouted behind them.

Hayward glanced over his shoulder and saw Logan standing at the corner with a gun trained on them.

Hayward was minded to take his chances and keep running, but ahead Dale and Gomez came round the corner with guns already drawn, having skirted around the hotel. In a resigned manner he stomped on for another few paces before stopping, but Ralston wove to either side as he sought a way past them.

Gomez thrust up a hand catching him beneath the chin and knocking him aside. Ralston hit the ground on his side and before he could recover, Dale dropped to his knees and dug his gun into the back of Ralston's neck.

'Don't struggle,' he muttered.

Ralston tensed, and when Logan shouted at Dale to shoot him, he looked at Hayward for help. Hayward moved forward preparing to risk charging at the gunmen, but Walcott followed Logan around the corner and raised a hand.

'As we agreed, you can deal with them,' he said. 'But only after they've answered my questions.'

Logan conceded his demand with a nod and so Dale dragged Ralston to his feet. With Gomez keeping a gun on Hayward, they followed Walcott.

When they passed Logan, he directed a triumphant glare at them, which they ignored as they were led into the hotel. They were taken through a kitchen and on to a corridor where an anxious bellhop was pacing back and forth before a closed door.

'Nobody knows,' he said.

'Except for the people you'll now tell,' Walcott said. He waited until the bellhop gulped. 'Just make sure those people aren't guests.'

He shooed the bellhop away and opened the door. Hayward went in first and came to a halt when a familiar scene confronted him.

A young woman lay beside the bed, blankets having been dragged off the bed to cover most of her body. The coverings that had been pulled aside revealed her sliced throat, her pale face and the blood that had pooled around her shoulders.

Ralston considered the scene in silence, leaving Hayward to turn to Walcott.

'You found her this morning?' he asked.

'I did. Then I heard that two men were asking about Malachi's show.'

'Why is that important?' Hayward kept his tone neutral although he already expected the answer.

'She's Penelope Galloway. Last night Malachi picked her from the audience to take part in his act. Later, Severin O'Hara left the music hall with her. She paid a heavy price for her mistake.'

'Just like Mary and Lucy,' Logan said.

His comment made his men bunch up in the corridor as they awaited instructions.

'This isn't our doing,' Ralston said. 'We've never seen this woman before.'

'A likely story,' Walcott said. 'Tell me the truth, or Logan will make you pay for this.'

Ralston jutted his jaw, as if he were considering his reply making Logan tense, but instead he used the distraction to grab the nearest man and push him backwards. As the man knocked into Walcott sending them both sprawling into the corridor wall, he grabbed the door and slammed it shut in everyone's faces.

While Ralston toppled furniture before the door, Hayward ran for the open window. He glanced down and dismissed the twenty-five foot drop down to the ground as being too far.

'Get out the window,' Ralston said, as

the door shook suggesting they didn't have enough time to tie blankets together. 'I'll follow.'

Hayward reckoned his badge would force Walcott to hear him out, but a thud sounded against the door as the men organized themselves, making Ralston jerk away and letting Hayward see into the corridor briefly.

Dale and Gomez were brandishing guns and so as Ralston slammed the door shut the imminent danger decided Hayward's next course of action. He sat on the sill and swung his legs over the edge as the door burst open, sending splintered wood flying, scattering furniture, and throwing Ralston aside.

As the men spilled on to the floor, Ralston got to his feet and so Hayward pressed his boots to the wall. Then, using the traction, he lowered himself until he was dangling.

He didn't have enough time to check on how far he would have to drop as a gunshot peeled out within the room. Then a shocked looking Ralston thrust his head out of the window.

Hayward released his grip and faster than he expected he slammed down to the ground and wheeled backwards into the opposite wall.

He had righted himself and was flexing his ankles to confirm he'd done no damage when up in the room a volley of gunshots thundered through the window and Ralston landed before him. As Ralston tumbled backward, like Hayward had done, Hayward noted the shots had clattered into the wall far above his head.

Hayward grabbed Ralston and checked he was fine. Then they set off for the main drag as above them, their attackers appeared at the window and uttered irritated grunts.

Dale and Gomez levelled guns on them, but in the confined space they got in each other's way and so when they fired their shots were wild. With the bullets tearing into the walls and ground behind them, Hayward and Ralston gained the corner.

Unfortunately, the stable was on the other side of the hotel and so when they reached the boardwalk they had to run past the hotel windows. They kept low and they were three paces from the main door when it flew open and one of their attackers emerged.

That man wasted valuable seconds peering around and Hayward made him pay for his slowness when he ran into him and knocked him on his back. Then he vaulted the body and with Ralston, he sprinted down the board-walk.

They ran past a mercantile with only the man he'd knocked over hobbling after them. Hayward was starting to think they'd get away when Ralston slapped an arm across his chest, alerting him to the fact that Patrick was now guarding the stable door.

'He must have doubled back,' Ralston murmured.

Hayward nodded. 'Then we have to try another way.'

When Patrick noticed them and

walked purposefully towards them, they turned away and hurried towards a concentration of people that was closing on the hotel.

With every step Hayward feared getting a bullet in the back, but they slipped into the throng without Patrick taking action. Overheard murmured comments confirmed the bellhop had spread the news about Penelope's death and that, along with the gunfire, was drawing people to the hotel.

When Hayward saw Logan emerge from the hotel to join the other pursuers, he got Ralston's attention and pointed at the law office, but Ralston shook his head.

'I'm not confiding in another lawman,' he said. 'I reckon when you're free, you stay free.'

Hayward was minded to argue, but Logan was already moving between them and the law office.

'Agreed,' he said and so they worked their way through the milling people who were craning their necks seeking a better view of the situation.

Within a minute, the crowd thinned out, but ahead another stream of people was moving away from the hotel towards the station. When he looked back, Logan was thirty paces behind them with Dale and Gomez spreading out seeking to trap them in a pincer-like movement.

So they hurried on into the midst of the next group of people. Promisingly, a train had drawn in and while it took on water, many of the passengers were wandering around on the platform.

'Where's the train heading?' Ralston asked the nearest man.

'Next stop Prudence,' the man replied before clambering up into a car.

As Malachi's show had moved on to Prudence, without comment Ralston and Hayward followed the man inside. They found a spare seat on the platform side of the train.

A minute passed quietly before Logan bustled on to the platform. While with irritated gestures he questioned people, on the train Ralston drew his hat down in a posture of seeking sleep until Hayward got his attention with a sharp intake of breath.

'Trouble?' Ralston asked.

'Yeah,' Hayward said. 'Logan's boarding the train.'

8

'You were late back last night,' Adam said when Severin joined him beside the campfire.

Severin smiled and wolfed down a spoonful of stew before he replied.

'Moving on every day has its advantages,' he said. 'I never miss an opportunity to enjoy my free time and tomorrow will be busy. We have one night to work out how we're going to stage an act that's even more dangerous than the most dangerous act ever performed.'

They had rested up a few hours out of Prudence beside a creek. The ground was flat and they were in a clear area with the firelight illuminating the creek and the surrounding scrub for dozens of yards.

Malachi was eating alone in the wagon he now shared only with Severin and himself, while Katherine and Florence were eating their meal standing up outside their wagon.

Both men ate in silence for a while until Adam glanced at Severin.

'It's not really dangerous, is it?' he asked.

'Two men standing ten paces apart and shooting each other, but both surviving only because they catch the bullet in their teeth.' Severin took another mouthful. 'Sounds dangerous to me.'

Adam finished his meal, giving Severin a chance to admit he was joking, but when he only considered him while chewing, he shook his head.

'Malachi abandoned the act in Carmon after that woman you left with said the bullet was real.'

'She apologized later.' Severin put his plate on the ground. 'So what do you think Malachi really does?'

'The gun is loaded with a bullet that the person from the audience sees, but you swap it for a fake gun.' Adam watched Severin frown, so he shrugged. 'Or it's a real gun with a blank cartridge. You fire, but Malachi already has a bullet in his mouth.'

'An interesting option.' Severin leaned forward. 'But the glass between us breaks.'

Adam winced, having forgotten about that aspect.

'The rope around the glass is burning and that shatters it.'

'At the precise moment I fire?'

'In that case you shoot something that's hard enough to break the glass but not tough enough to reach Malachi.' Adam looked aloft as he considered the conversations he'd overheard and the preparations he'd seen. 'Such as the paraffin wax Florence rubs on the rope.'

'That's a dangerous option.' Severin stood. 'But then again, this is the most dangerous act ever performed.'

As Severin walked to Malachi's wagon to collect his plate, Adam considered that statement, wondering if it confirmed his guess had been right. He decided he hadn't got all the details, but he'd been close to the truth and that let him become impressed again, as what they did was as dangerous as they claimed, despite the trick element.

When Severin had collected everyone's plates, Malachi emerged and he and Severin talked in low tones while glancing at him. Then, with a smile on his lips, Malachi came over.

'Severin tells me you have another theory about my act,' he said.

'I have, and it's a good one.'

Malachi smiled. Then he slapped him on the shoulder and ushered him to join him before the fire.

'In that case, I reckon you're ready to take on a larger role in Prudence.'

Thirty minutes later, the group was ready to perform their first rehearsal of the bullet catch showdown. Severin had marked out a square to represent the stage while the sisters had placed the main props in their usual positions.

Malachi had given Adam his lines, although during his performance two nights from now he would have to react to any situation that may develop. He would fulfil both audience participation parts, so he would confirm the wax bullets were genuine and stay on stage so that Malachi could make him disappear.

They hadn't seen Derrick since his failed attempt to kill Malachi in Carmon, but he must know he'd failed. With Adam on hand to ensure the bullets weren't switched again, if Derrick followed them to Prudence, everyone reckoned he wouldn't be able to do anything other than to cause mischief, as he'd done in Bear Creek.

As Adam had planned to do in Carmon, a saloon girl would accompany him, and as before in the rehearsal Florence took on that role with enthusiasm. She giggled and proclaimed that she wondered who would dare go up on stage, and so to impress her Adam raised a hand.

Malachi reported that he wouldn't pick him immediately and he'd quiz two other men about their knowledge of guns. He'd reject both of them as not being knowledgeable enough and so by the time he moved on to Adam, the audience would be restless. Accordingly, he would relent and accept Adam after only learning his name.

Adam stood awkwardly beside Malachi as Katherine brought out the guns. Then he replied as was required as he verified the bullets loaded in both guns were real.

He picked out one bullet to show to the imaginary audience. Then, improvising, he put the slug between his teeth and pretended to bite down on it while shaking his head in wonderment at the impossibility of the act to be performed.

This made Florence laugh and after considering, Malachi nodded with approval. Then, with his part of the act finished, he moved to the back of the stage area to join Katherine where he watched Malachi mark out his precise measurements.

Now he knew the nature of the trick he appreciated the risks involved.

Malachi had to ensure the bullets were solid enough and had enough charge to smash the glass, but not enough to harm the target.

It was only while Katherine was positioning the hoop that for the first time Adam spotted an element of the trick that nobody had revealed. Malachi and Severin would stand on either side of the hoop in a position that was slightly off line.

They weren't planning to shoot at each other and so even if the coating on the wax bullets proved more resilient than expected, the debris still wouldn't hit either man. He couldn't blame them for this precaution and so even though this was a rehearsal and they wouldn't complete the showdown, Adam was so enraptured by the performance he stood quietly.

Malachi had made two marks where he and Severin were to stand and to increase tension both men paced around those marks before they settled down. They faced each other with their guns aimed downwards.

Now he'd spotted the hoop wasn't directly between them he could see that both men would fire over their target's shoulder. Malachi would aim at the safe into which he'd disappear later while Severin would fire at the board that Katherine stood against during the knife trick.

No wax should survive to make a mark and it was unlikely to be noticed if it did. That thought made him consider the safe.

The safe had been placed between the wagons, but tomorrow night it would be at the side of the stage. It had been constructed using thin timber so it could be moved easily and if the wax bullet reached it, it could break through.

He was wondering if he should mention his concern when, to his amazement, the safe wobbled. He blinked, thinking the tension had made his vision play tricks on him, but again the safe rocked.

He swayed to the right seeking to see more of the safe so he could work out what was making it move. The new position let him see through the crack between the door and the jamb.

Something was moving inside.

With a flinch Adam realized that someone had crawled in through the small door at the back. As everyone in the group was visible, he stepped forward.

'Derrick's back,' he said, his voice cutting through the silence.

Malachi and Severin swirled round to face him. Before he could point out where he suspected Derrick was hiding a gunshot roared.

As both men were moving, the shot missed and they both survived intact, although Malachi twitched suggesting he had been the intended target and the shot had been close. Adam was the only one who was armed effectively and so he hurried across the stage area.

When he reached the safe, the small door at the back was swinging. He carried on between the wagons and saw Derrick's back as he hurried towards the safety of the shadows.

They had stopped in a clear area and in parts the surrounding undergrowth was waist high, so in the dark Derrick would be able to hide with ease. Adam sped up, but Derrick was still ten yards ahead of him as he sprinted into the undergrowth.

Raised voices sounded behind him as Malachi and the others tried to work out what had happened. Adam couldn't hear any sign of them joining him in the pursuit, but with his head down he still hurried into the undergrowth after Derrick.

Several boulders were ahead and Derrick didn't appear to be as familiar with the terrain as Adam was as he wasted valuable seconds working out which path to take to get by them. In the end he ran between two large rocks.

When Adam reached the rocks, his quarry was only three paces ahead, his form indistinct in the gloom. Beyond the rocks the undergrowth to the right was dense while the creek was to the left.

Derrick ran towards the creek and before they reached another large boulder, Derrick slowed, perhaps from uncertainty of what lay beyond, letting Adam gain on him. He thrust out an arm to grab him.

Derrick leapt around the boulder avoiding Adam's grasping hand. So as Adam swung around the rock, he had no doubt Derrick's capture was seconds away.

Two paces on, Adam stomped to a halt, staring ahead with his heart thudding from exertion and surprise. Derrick had gone.

Twenty yards ahead was the creek and sufficient firelight from the camp illuminated the near by terrain to show the area was deserted.

A firm shove to the side sent Adam sprawling and he'd hit the ground before he worked out that Derrick had known the terrain better than he'd shown. He'd hidden in a shadow-laden indentation in the boulder to surprise him.

With a grunt of triumph, Derrick leapt on him. The two men rolled over each other, and when they came to rest, Adam was lying on his back and Derrick was straddling him with his gun levelled down on his chest.

Adam tried to buck him, but Derrick had settled his weight firmly on him.

'Stop struggling or I'll kill you,' Derrick demanded.

Adam heaved an irritated sigh, but he stilled.

'When you knocked me out in Carmon, you claimed you were saving my life,' he said.

Derrick shrugged. 'I gave you your chance. You didn't take it.'

'Except I did. I've survived, as has Malachi.'

'Only because you saved him.'

'And I've done it twice now. Perhaps if I'd been working for the magic show three years ago, I'd have stopped you killing Jubal Jackson, too.'

Derrick snorted, but voices sounded near by and so he changed position to lessen the weight he pressed down on him.

'You're not as clever as you think you are.' Derrick laughed, his teeth and eyes bright in the dark. 'You have no proof Jubal died, or that he even existed in the first place, but then again if you were clever enough to figure out the truth, Malachi wouldn't have picked you.'

'He once picked you, too.'

'He did, but he didn't plan on me working out what he's been hiding in plain sight while everyone thought he was only a magician. Take this as your last warning: leave Malachi's show while you still can.'

'Threats won't work on me,' Adam said.

Before Adam finished speaking, Derrick leapt to his feet. He glanced in the direction of the approaching voices and then backed away.

'That was no threat,' he said as he slipped away into the darkness. 'If you go to Prudence, you will die.'

9

'Keep walking and stay with the crowd,' Hayward said.

'We can't stay with them forever,' Ralston said. 'Everyone's got somewhere to go to.'

Reluctantly Hayward nodded. On the train they'd stayed in a crowded car and so Logan hadn't made a move on them.

Around twenty people had disembarked at Prudence and they'd slipped into the centre of that group, but now those people were spreading out as they sought out hotels.

'Agreed. The moment Logan gets close, we run for the law office.'

'You're still determined that we avoid sorting out this mess ourselves?'

'Logan killed a lawman. That's all I intend to tell the law. Once that's sorted out, we'll deal with Severin together.'

Ralston said nothing for several

strides. Then he provided a firm nod while pointing ahead.

'Unless we get the chance to deal with him first.'

Three buildings away stood a music hall and a notice outside announced that tomorrow night Malachi would be performing. Tonight's show had just ended, and when two men emerged to open doors, people spilled out on to the road while chatting about the night's entertainment.

Hayward glanced over his shoulder and noted Logan and his two men were walking fifty yards behind them while eyeing the commotion with irritation.

'We know where Malachi will be for the next two nights. That'll give us enough time to find Severin.'

'I don't need time.' Ralston pointed at a man and woman who were walking arm in arm through the door. 'That's Severin O'Hara.'

Hayward nodded and so, with their next actions decided, he put Logan from his mind and waded into the throng. The crowd swept them along and even if they'd wanted to seek a different direction, they'd have found it impossible.

They were thirty paces behind their quarries, but at least two dozen people were between them and they couldn't get closer as they were bustled along to the saloon beside the music hall.

Although the Broken Arrow was a large building, it couldn't cater for all the people and so Hayward hoped Logan might be kept outside, but Ralston dashed that hope when he pointed over his shoulder.

Twenty feet back and trapped in the doorway amidst a block of people, Logan was glaring at them. Dale and Gomez were barging customers aside, but with humanity pressing in on every side they couldn't make headway.

'Logan showed in Carmon that he won't act when lots of people are around,' Hayward said, shouting to be heard over the hubbub. 'But he might take advantage of the confusion, so we should head for the law office. It's opposite the saloon.'

'I've seen something better.' Ralston pointed, the action knocking the man in front of him and making him grumble. 'Sheriff Simmons is at the bar.'

Hayward smiled, and when Ralston returned the smile, they moved towards Simmons, making Logan redouble his efforts and shove people aside as he tried to reach them. Hayward and Ralston failed to make headway and worse, the mass of people moved them past the bar.

Ahead, the only people who moved against the tide were their quarries and the couple managed to snake around several customers to reach the stairs. With playful hugs and giggles, they hurried up the stairs and out of view accentuating Hayward and Ralston's problem of whether to speak to Simmons or waylay them.

'You deal with Severin,' Hayward said, tapping Ralston's shoulder. 'I'll talk to Simmons.'

Ralston nodded and so they looked for the best route forward, but they'd yet to move when Logan blasted a high gunshot, the sound quelling the excited chatter. Then, despite the crush, the people split apart like tight cloth being sliced by a knife, creating a corridor with Logan standing at the end.

'The chase ends here,' he shouted.

As people struggled to move away from the potential gunfight, Hayward gestured at the unarmed Ralston to join the fleeing people. Ralston shook his head, and so Hayward used the gesture to disguise him drawing his gun.

The moment the weapon cleared leather he turned at the hip, his speed fuelled on by a desire not to make the mistake he'd made in Bear Creek of letting a bad situation develop.

Several stragglers were still between him and Logan and so he picked out Dale and fired. His shot hammered into Dale's chest while in a reflex action Dale fired, but his gun was still aimed low and his shot tore into the floor.

Dale dropped to his knees where he glared at Hayward with his mouth opening to shout a taunt of defiance, but he toppled over on to his chest leaving it unsaid.

The gunshot made the crowd surge with one group swallowing up Logan while another group spread out to leave Gomez standing in clear space.

While Gomez struggled to right himself after the sudden movement, Hayward dispatched him with a low shot to the guts that made him double over before he ploughed face first to the saloon floor.

With an angry roar, Logan barged customers aside using a mixture of his left fist, both shoulders, and several kicks. By the time he'd cleared enough space to give him an uninterrupted view of Hayward, three customers were lying sprawled on the floor and he stood over them glaring across the saloon at Hayward.

'I'm Sheriff Simmons and Deputy Kennedy is here, too,' a loud voice proclaimed behind Hayward. 'Put down your guns while you still can.'

Logan ignored the sheriff's demand and he snapped up his gun arm. He fired, but the shot winged over Hayward's shoulder and clattered into a wall making the customers around Hayward dive to the floor.

In retaliation, Hayward picked Logan out with his gun. Driven on by the memory of his dead boss lying on the ground, before Logan could fire again he hammered a deadly shot into Logan's forehead that cracked his head back.

Logan swayed for a moment before toppling over, adding to the confusion of bodies and people lying around him. When Hayward noted that the three gunmen were still, he turned to the sheriff.

Simmons had clambered up on to the bar to look over the customers' heads and he'd turned his gun on Hayward. So Hayward raised his gun arm to aim upwards while raising his other hand in a show of surrender.

He sensed that Ralston was moving away from him. As there was no reason for anyone to assume they were together, he didn't look at him as he sought to resolve their other problem.

'You'll get no trouble from me,' he said.

'I'm pleased to hear it.' Simmons jumped down off the bar and in a room that was starting to bustle again, he worked his way through the customers. 'But make your story a good one.'

'I'm a deputy sheriff from Bear Creek,' Hayward said when Simmons reached him. He pointed at Logan's body. 'That man killed Sheriff Washington. And another killer's upstairs.'

To back up his comment, Hayward holstered his gun. The two men considered each other until Simmons gave a sharp nod and so both men turned to the stairs.

Ralston had already reached the top of the stairs where he was peering at the scene below. The moment he saw them coming towards them, he headed down the corridor.

With Simmons at Hayward's side, the customers moved aside and after taking the stairs two at a time they reached the corridor as Ralston stopped beside a door.

Ralston put a finger to his lips, but Simmons didn't mask the sound of his heavy footfalls and he took the lead in pushing through the door.

Ralston and Hayward followed him in to be confronted by the sight of two shocked people standing by a bed and locked in an embrace.

'What are you doing?' the woman demanded.

'We're saving your life,' Hayward said. 'That's what we're doing.'

* * *

'That's one hell of a story,' Sheriff Simmons said.

Adam Clements watched Simmons pace back and forth across the law office while he collected his thoughts giving him time to introduce himself to the men who had accused Severin.

The bodies of three men were lying in a corner of the law office wrapped in blankets while Severin O'Hara was under arrest in a cell.

'You had a lucky escape from Malachi's show, Adam,' Hayward Knight said.

'So people keep telling me,' Adam said. 'But I don't believe it yet.'

'And I'll take a while before I believe what I've heard,' Sheriff Simmons said. 'After Hayward's handed in his gun, you folks can leave the office. You'll all stay in town until I'm satisfied you've told the truth.'

As that last order had been directed at him as well as the other men, Adam headed out of the law office in a state of shock. He waited on the boardwalk for Hayward Knight and Ralston Hope to join him.

'While you're in town, look out for Derrick Fox,' Adam said. 'He's hell-bent on ruining Malachi's show, if there's still a show for him to ruin.'

Adam sighed. Prior to Severin's arrest, Malachi's group had been in good spirits.

After his failed attempt to kill Malachi, they hadn't seen Derrick again. When they'd arrived in Prudence, everyone's gloomy predictions about the aftermath of the events in Carmon hadn't materialized.

Walcott Quinn hadn't passed on information to Prudence's music hall owner Thaddeus Kemp. So they would enjoy two nights of sell-out performances ending with a large pay-out and the promise of more bookings elsewhere.

That no longer looked likely. When he'd left Malachi, he'd been trying to assure Thaddeus that even without Severin he could still put on a show.

'Don't waste time worrying about the show,' Hayward said. 'You shouldn't risk returning to Malachi.'

'But I have to tell him what's

happened so we can work out how we'll prove Severin's innocence.'

Hayward snorted an incredulous laugh. 'I applaud your loyalty to Malachi and Severin, but you have to accept the fact that wherever Malachi's show goes, it leaves behind a trail of bodies.'

'There could be plenty of explanations for that.' Adam waved his arms as he struggled to find one. 'Malachi and his people are dedicated to performing magic. They're careful and they get every detail right. Severin wouldn't leave obvious clues that lead back to him.'

Hayward looked aloft. 'So you're saying Derrick's the culprit, not Severin?'

'I can only tell you what I've seen. Derrick's a violent drunkard who's trying to kill Malachi while Severin's always been friendly to me.'

Hayward and Ralston glanced at each other and both men nodded.

'We understand what you're saying. We'll keep an open mind.'

'Do that.' Adam shrugged and turned

away. 'And while you do what you have to do, I have to find out if I still have a job.'

'Be careful,' Hayward called after him, but as Derrick had offered such a sentiment last night Adam waved a dismissive hand and carried on walking.

He took a long route back to the music hall letting him organize his thoughts, but he was no clearer about who to believe when he joined Malachi in the back room of the music hall.

When he reported what he'd found out, everyone reacted with horror and bewilderment. Even though they earned a living through playacting, Adam accepted their reaction as being honest.

'This is terrible,' Florence said with a glance at Katherine, who was so speechless she could only gulp. 'Severin would never harm anyone. The killer has to be Derrick.'

'I agree,' Adam said. 'But until he's caught, the situation will look bad for Severin.'

The four people sat in silence with

everyone looking at Malachi, awaiting his response, but he kept his silence for several minutes before, with a cough, he spoke up.

'Derrick couldn't have expected Severin to be blamed for his crimes,' he said. 'So he'll strike again, either at me or at another woman. We have to draw him out before that happens, but it'll be hard now we no longer have a show.'

'Only the bullet catch showdown is affected,' Adam said. 'The rest of the act can continue as normal.'

'Except everything works around the showdown. Without it we have only card tricks and disappearances, and after the disastrous performance in Carmon, we can't afford to present another weak act.'

The group sat silently, this time for longer than before until Katherine spoke up for the first time.

'The showdown could still continue,' she said, looking at Adam. 'He knows the secret of the bullet catch now. He could take Severin's place.'

'You want me to catch a bullet with my teeth?' Adam murmured, his voice gaining in strength as the idea captured his imagination.

'Only the bravest souls can survive the most dangerous act in the world,' Malachi said, leaning forward eagerly. 'Are you one of them?'

'Derrick warned me that if I went to Prudence, I would die.' Adam smiled. 'I reckon I should prove him wrong.'

10

'Derrick's not hiding behind the stage,' Ralston said when he joined Hayward.

'He's not at the sides either,' Hayward said. He peered around the curtain at the gathering audience. 'And we'd have heard by now if he'd joined the audience.'

Ralston nodded and returned to his position on the other side of the stage, while Hayward folded his arms and leaned back against the wall to await Derrick's ploy, assuming Adam had been correct and Derrick had followed the show to Prudence.

This morning, when they'd tried to piece together the situation with Sheriff Simmons, Ralston remembered seeing Malachi's female assistant Florence in the act four years ago, but he hadn't noticed Derrick. On the other hand Derrick's role would have been anonymous and only Derrick appeared to have a grievance, even if they were unsure what it was.

Although Simmons accepted their story that Derrick could have killed the women, he hadn't released Severin. Throughout the day nobody had seen any sign of Derrick and so Simmons had posted Deputy Kennedy at the door while other deputies mingled in with the music hall audience.

The promise of seeing the most dangerous act ever performed had drawn the largest audience Hayward had ever seen. Prudence's music hall was twice the size of Bear Creek's, and thirty minutes before the performance most of the seats had been filled.

Earlier, the only door at the back of the music hall had been barred ensuring the only way in was to accompany the audience through the front door. As Derrick wasn't amongst them, his only other option, if he planned to kill Malachi tonight, was to have sneaked inside already.

Hayward and Ralston had taken it upon themselves to help Simmons end this situation. Malachi hadn't appreciated their endeavours, as they provided an unwanted distraction to an act that had already been dangerous before the recent hasty revision.

Accordingly, Adam paced around nervously while Malachi listened to Hayward's update on the situation without interest.

'If everything is to your satisfaction, you can join the audience now,' Malachi said sarcastically when Hayward had finished.

'It'd be safer if we were to stay back here.'

'If you haven't checked adequately, check again before you leave.' He considered Hayward, but when he returned his gaze impassively, he tapped the safe at the side of the stage. 'I have secrets to protect and they're more important than my life.'

'That's your decision. If Derrick kills you, that'll tell us where he is and he won't get far.'

Having got in a satisfying last word, Hayward walked across the stage and collected Ralston, who wasn't concerned about them having to abandon the plan to stay backstage.

'Unless Derrick can get through a barred door he won't try anything tonight,' Ralston said.

'Which begs the question, what will he do instead?'

They both winced, acknowledging the alternatives were equally troubling. He might kill another woman, or he might flee and leave Severin to take the blame for the murders he'd committed.

So in a more subdued frame of mind than that displayed by the excitable audience, they took up their seats on the end of the front row. After a few minutes, Simmons joined them and confirmed he'd checked with his deputies and Derrick hadn't been seen.

When Simmons returned to the back of the music hall, there was nothing left for them to do other than to watch and wait.

Thirty minutes later the show started. As it turned out, tonight there were two warm-up acts.

Firstly a young woman wearing short petticoats sang campfire songs around a pile of wood coated in flimsy red paper to simulate flames. She got catcalls, which she rebuffed with bawdy jokes suggesting she was a regular.

Afterwards acrobats tumbled and rolled around the stage and although they generated less enthusiasm than the singer had done, Hayward was impressed with their athleticism.

Then Malachi arrived and despite having seen his performance in Bear Creek, Hayward enjoyed watching him entrance the audience with his dexterity and with his ready wit that built on the comments hecklers shouted out. So, when Malachi made Florence appear in a previously empty safe, Ralston leaned towards him.

'Perhaps I was wrong to suspect these people,' he said, speaking loudly over the applause. 'I thought Florence was in the act four years ago, but I don't reckon she's the same woman now.'

Hayward nodded. 'Which means we only know for sure that Severin was in Bear Creek when Mary was killed.'

'So why is Derrick trying to kill Malachi?'

'I don't know.' Hayward frowned. 'But if he has a reason, it makes me wonder whose life we should be trying to save.'

★ ★ ★

When Malachi reached Adam's part of the act, underneath the mask, Adam's face was roasting. Even though he was standing in a cool spot beside the stage, droplets of sweat dripped down his neck and pooled against his collar.

He was still determined to complete the performance even though they'd practised it only twice. Now he understood the procedure, he knew the risks he would take and they relied on trusting that care had been taken over the preparation.

So he was relieved that Malachi had kept a tight control over this process. Earlier he'd recruited Sheriff Simmons to be the witness, ensuring there were no unpredictable elements. So when Malachi called for Simmons to come up on stage and verify the bullets were real, the lawman accepted with a world-weary sigh.

While Katherine brought out the guns, the lawman played along with the required responses while keeping one eye on the audience. With Simmons's devotion to duty giving him additional confidence, Adam stopped looking for trouble and concentrated on his role.

That still didn't stop the sweat from slicking his face. When Malachi gave him his cue to come on stage, he raised the mask and wiped his cheeks. Then, with a deep breath, he slipped the flattened slug into his mouth and tucked it under his tongue before he went out.

Severin's role had been to stand

quietly and enigmatically to build up tension while Malachi acted in a more animated manner. So Adam was thankful he had only to pick out the mark Malachi had made for him and look straight ahead.

He ignored the audience, which was easy to do with the mask restricting his vision, and tried to instil the feeling this was another rehearsal. During their practice runs, they hadn't fired the guns as the wax slugs were hard to make and Malachi had only enough for the two-night performance.

The cold lump of metal in his mouth felt larger than it had felt in his hand and he swirled it around his mouth as he tried to find a comfortable position. His ministrations sent it to the back of his throat where a gag reflex made him swallow and he had to cough which almost made the bullet fly from his lips.

He looked around feeling concerned that someone had spotted his discomfort, but Malachi was checking the hoop was in the right position. Adam took the near disaster as a warning for him to pay attention to what was happening rather than trying to still his nerves.

He checked he was in the right position and with the slug trapped between his teeth he stood tall. He ensured the safe was behind the hoop where it could safely deal with any residue from the bullet, if it reached that far.

'Do you accept my solemn declaration that if I kill the other man,' Malachi asked Simmons, 'no crime will have been committed?'

'I do,' Simmons said.

Adam provided the same declaration, although the bullet in his mouth made him struggle to speak. While he resolved to practice speaking with something in his mouth before tomorrow, Simmons joined Katherine at the back of the stage.

With the audience silencing, Malachi took up his position. During the aborted rehearsal yesterday, Malachi and Severin had increased tension by adopting their positions and seemingly changing their minds several times.

As this was his first performance, Malachi had agreed they would fire at the first opportunity, which would come when Katherine tapped a finger against the brand for the fifth time.

Accordingly, Katherine lit the rope and stood back, holding the brand with her index finger raised. Behind Malachi and off stage in a position where she was out of sight from everyone else, Florence appeared in the shadows.

She gave him a cheery wave before she adopted a serious posture and took a pace sideways to move herself out of his firing range, even if he aimed badly.

A few moments later the flames spread around the rope providing, Adam now knew, an eye-catching distraction. That was his cue to cock the six-shooter and raise his arm to take aim through the hoop.

He picked out his target of a rose-shaped decoration on the safe, which was a point four feet away from

Malachi's left shoulder. This position was far enough away from his apparent target to be safe, but close enough to make it look from the audience as if they were facing each other in a showdown.

He ignored everything but his target and Katherine's finger, knowing a mistake could cost him his life and trusting Malachi was being equally careful.

Katherine tapped her finger, making him tense his trigger finger. She tapped again as something moved at the corner of his vision.

He ignored the movement, but as she tapped for a third time, the movement came again. This time he flicked his gaze away, but he saw nothing other than to note that Florence was no longer visible.

Katherine tapped again while Adam struggled to overcome his nervousness by staring at his target of the safe. Then Katherine tapped for the final time and, with him concentrating intensely, he fired.

Gunfire rattled and a hammer blow slammed against his chest, making him drop to his knees, his breath stolen away and his chest feeling as if it'd been cracked in two. His confused senses told him he'd seen a flash of light off stage, but the pain was too much for him to even think about it.

His head thudded against the stage floor as he fell on to his side. He looked at Simmons who was nodding with a knowing expression that said he'd worked out how they'd performed the trick.

On the other side of the stage, Malachi was also lying in a crumpled heap. He wasn't moving as, seemingly from a great distance, the audience roared with consternation.

'It's not a trick,' Adam gasped. 'I've been shot.'

He wasn't sure if he'd spoken aloud. The stage was darkening and he could no longer see Katherine or Simmons.

He felt more alone than he'd ever done.

11

'Adam's dead,' Sheriff Simmons declared.

Malachi nodded, his expression shocked, and everybody else on stage lowered their heads while the audience chatter grew louder as they jostled for a better view of the scene. The doors were guarded after Simmons had ordered the music hall to remain closed, but so far nobody had wanted to leave.

'Accident?' Ralston asked, leaning towards Hayward.

'Either that or a murder made to look like an accident,' Hayward said. 'But I don't know how the trick was supposed to work to know for sure.'

Ralston nodded, while Simmons gestured for them to join him on stage. When they'd clambered up, Deputy Kennedy returned to report the door at the back was still barred on the inside.

Ralston and Hayward knelt beside

Adam's body. He had spent only a few minutes with this man, but his death had shocked him almost as much as Sheriff Washington's had.

Adam had joined the act in Bear Creek and he had appeared a decent man who perhaps knew more than he was aware of about the activities within the magic show.

Although as this incident didn't help to prove Severin's innocence, he presumed Simmons would keep him locked up, so it was likely the show was no more as Malachi no longer had enough help to continue.

Accordingly, when Florence joined him and knelt on the other side of Adam's body, her shocked expression registered she knew the show was over.

'Malachi showed him what to do,' she said. 'I don't know what went wrong.'

Hayward shrugged. 'I guess this proves nobody can catch a bullet with their teeth.'

She removed Adam's mask. Protruding through his lips was a slug, seemingly having been fired and caught.

'Except he did.' Her voice caught and she had to stifle a sob. She turned away to stand with her shoulders heaving before she scurried off the stage.

'That clarifies one part of the trick,' Ralston said. 'But it doesn't explain how it went so badly wrong.'

'The only thing we know for sure is that was no accident,' Simmons said, coming over to join them.

'Why are you so sure?'

Simmons pointed at the body and then at the hoop in the centre of the stage.

'From where I was standing, I could see they weren't aiming at each other, which means Malachi didn't shoot Adam.'

Simmons waited until both men nodded. Then he moved to the front of the stage, and when he beckoned Deputy Kennedy to let the audience leave, Hayward reckoned they were free to see what else they could learn.

He and Ralston considered the props. They found nothing of interest until they examined the safe behind Malachi, which was flimsier than it looked with a small door at the back.

With the first inkling of an idea coming to him, Hayward stood in the safe and gestured for Ralston to close the door.

Light still filtered inside and he soon located several holes including one that was large enough to accommodate a gun barrel.

★ ★ ★

'I'm still keeping Severin O'Hara under arrest,' Sheriff Simmons said when Hayward and Ralston visited him in the morning.

'I know last night didn't prove Severin's innocence,' Hayward said. 'But he didn't kill Adam and — '

'I'm not interested in your opinion, just in the facts of where you've been and what you've been doing.'

Hayward and Ralston glanced at each other and shrugged before they both came up to the desk to consider Simmons, who was no longer acting in the genial manner he'd adopted with them last night.

'We've been asking around, but we've found nothing out, yet.'

'And you won't do because you'll stop asking questions. This isn't your town and this isn't your investigation.'

Hayward offered a placating smile the sheriff didn't return, and so Ralston took over.

'Yesterday you welcomed our help,' he said. 'Today you want nothing to do with us.'

'Yesterday you rode into town and the first I knew of you was seeing you shoot up three men. Then you were at the music hall when another man was killed.'

'We tried to work out what had happened and we came up with a plausible explanation,' Hayward said. He watched Simmons raise an eyebrow with an exasperated expression that said he'd retort to any objection they made, and so he lowered his voice. 'Why are you now suspicious of us?'

Simmons considered both men, his silence suggesting he was hoping they'd continue making guesses about the reason for his anger, but when they said nothing he leaned back in his chair.

'I confirmed the details you gave me and they're worrying. In every town you visited a woman's body turned up, and you shot up the men who were seeking retribution for one of those deaths.'

'I shot up Logan because he killed a lawman.'

Simmons smiled triumphantly as if they'd now mentioned the reason for his antipathy.

'I got an answer back about that, too. Sheriff Washington is dead, but nobody knows about the circumstances other than that several men left town in a hurry afterwards, and those men include you.'

Hayward conceded Simmons's right to be suspicious with a frown.

'Perhaps we should return to Bear

Creek and explain ourselves.'

'You're going nowhere until I get some answers. Act suspiciously and I'll throw you in a cell.'

Simmons turned his head away with a determined motion that ended their conversation, leaving the two men to head outside. They said nothing more until they were standing at the bar in the Broken Arrow saloon.

'I made a mistake when I joined you,' Hayward said with a sigh. 'I had my duty back there and instead I tried to solve crimes that weren't my business.'

'Maybe you did,' Ralston said. 'But this has become your business now and we can work out what's going on.'

'The only people we can question without raising Simmons's suspicions are Malachi and Florence.' Hayward hunched over his drink. 'And last night they were so upset I doubt they'll remember anything useful.'

Ralston sipped his drink while smiling for the first time today.

'That's your trouble. You think too

152

much like a lawman.'

'I've got no choice about that. Have you got a better idea?'

'Sure. We stop following one step behind whoever killed the women and Adam, and make something happen.' Ralston swirled his whiskey. 'Such as reviving the bullet catch showdown tonight.'

'One of Malachi's assistants is in jail and the other one's dead.'

Ralston winked. 'Then he'll need a new assistant.'

Hayward gave Ralston an incredulous look, but Ralston returned it levelly and so despite his misgivings, fifteen minutes later they were sitting in a back room at the music hall facing an equally sceptical Malachi.

'I own the act,' Malachi said with a sombre tone. 'I won't reveal its secret to outsiders.'

'If you want to continue with the act, you have no choice,' Ralston said.

Malachi paced around the assembled props for his performance, the casual way they'd been strewn about suggesting he no longer cared about them. He moved aside a dirty spade that had been propped against a chair and sat down to face them.

'The man who taught me the bullet catch died performing the act. If I involve you, it'll be after another unfortunate death. If the act were to kill again, I couldn't live with that and so I can only pass on the secret to someone who knows what they're doing.'

Malachi leaned forward to consider them, his narrow-eyed look conveying he didn't deem them proficient enough.

'We're familiar with using guns and more importantly we've seen the act, and we reckon we know how you do it.'

'A young man said the same thing to me recently. He's now dead.' Malachi spread his hands and leaned back. 'So why don't you tell me what you're really after?'

'We want to catch the man who's killing the women in the towns you visit,' Hayward said.

'We both saw the bodies,' Ralston added. 'But only I was accused of killing them.'

'Ah,' Malachi said, his short exclamation of surprise being the first reaction Hayward had seen him make that he trusted. 'My aloofness is merely my stage persona. I want whoever is doing this to be brought to justice, too.'

Ralston nodded. 'We believe that whoever killed Adam is also killing the women, which suggests Derrick is the most likely culprit. Help us to find him.'

'Letting you participate in the bullet catch show-down won't necessarily achieve your aims. It'll just give Derrick another chance to kill me.' Malachi pondered for a moment and then smiled. 'On the other hand, throwing down a challenge to a man who apparently likes challenges might force him into the open.'

Ralston and Hayward both smiled.

'And who better to catch a man who hides in plain sight than a man who's the master of hiding the truth in plain sight.'

'Who indeed?' Malachi said.

12

'Eagle,' Ralston said.

He smiled when Hayward raised his hand to show he'd guessed the outcome of the coin flick correctly.

After some debate, Malachi had agreed that tonight one of them could participate in the bullet catch showdown with him by taking Severin's and then Adam's role. So it was debatable whether winning was a good result and accordingly Ralston grabbed Hayward's hand and examined his sleeve.

Hayward laughed when he caught on to what he was doing.

'I haven't learnt any magic tricks yet,' he said. 'You really did call that correctly.'

Having decided who would take the lead, they headed back to the music hall. They had agreed to meet up with Malachi four hours before that night's performance, but as it turned out Malachi wasn't waiting for them.

Florence walked them through the procedure but without Malachi's help the rehearsal was lacklustre, giving Hayward no confidence Ralston would be able to perform an act that was clearly dangerous.

'How much longer is Malachi going to be?' Ralston asked when they'd completed the rehearsal, his irritated expression showing he was of the same mind as Hayward was.

'He's still depressed,' Florence said with a tense smile. 'In fact I've never seen him so distraught.'

'He sounded enthusiastic earlier.'

'That was before the sheriff spoke with him. Simmons doesn't want to risk a repeat of last night's events and he's banned the bullet catch showdown.' She looked around nervously, as if she hoped Malachi would appear. 'I thought Malachi would have returned by now with better news. As he hasn't, it's not certain there'll be a show tonight.'

Florence flopped down on the end of the stage in a resigned manner and so Hayward drew Ralston aside.

'Perhaps we need to speak to Simmons and persuade him this is the right way to end this matter,' he said.

Ralston laughed. 'I agree. After all, this is for just one night. I don't want to make a career out of catching bullets.'

Hayward agreed with this sentiment and so they left Florence to mooch around the stage and headed to the law office. The building was on the other side of the bank and when Hayward peered through the window, all was quiet inside.

Ralston tried the door and on finding it open he went in. Hayward followed him inside and confirmed the office was deserted.

As it was clear Malachi wasn't here, Hayward turned away meaning to go in search of the sheriff, but Ralston dallied to consider a pile of documents that were lying on the floor. In the otherwise tidy office, they looked out of place and they appeared to have been swept off the desk.

With a bemused expression on his face Ralston headed to the jailhouse door, which he pushed lightly. When the door edged open, he caught Hayward's eye before pushing it fully open.

He slipped inside and a moment later a strangulated gasp sounded, a sound that was so unexpected Hayward was unsure if Ralston had made it until a crunch sounded, as of someone falling over.

Hayward hurried across the office and pressed his back to the wall beside the jailhouse door. When he heard no further sounds coming from within, he hurried in, keeping low.

His foresight saved him from a wild swipe that had been aimed at head height, but which whistled through the air above his back. Alerted now to where Ralston's assailant was, Hayward turned to find Derrick Fox was standing before him.

Derrick was off-balance while Ralston lay on the floor at his feet. Outside the furthest cell Sheriff Simmons was lying on his chest while the nearest cell door was swinging open.

Inside Severin sat propped up against the bars, doubled over and clutching his bloodied side. Hayward didn't give Derrick time to regain his footing and he grabbed his jacket and repaid him for his treatment of Ralston by throwing him at the wall.

Derrick raised his arms to deflect the impact, but he still stumbled away where he received a thump in the side that made him grunt before Hayward kicked his legs out from under him.

Hayward stood over him and Derrick took his time in getting to one knee, but then, seemingly regaining his strength, he kicked off from the floor. As he rose up, he hammered a shoulder into Hayward's chest and carried him backwards for several paces until he thudded into the cell bars.

When Derrick released him, Hayward

noted that Ralston was looking past him with a worried expression on his face. The direction of Ralston's gaze told Hayward he should move to the left, which let him avoid the cell door Derrick swung towards him.

As the door clattered against the cell bars and rebounded, Derrick stormed forward. This time Hayward wasn't able to avoid his assailant and a solid blow with a bunched fist thudded into his ear, knocking him aside.

He went sprawling on to his knees where he shook himself. Then he slapped his hands on the floor to brace himself before rolling aside, but his quick action wasn't required, as his assailant hadn't followed through with a further attack.

He froze, unsure why Derrick hadn't used his advantage, but movement at the back of the jailhouse told Hayward what had happened a moment before Simmons spoke up. The lawman had drawn his gun stealthily and he was now lying on his chest with his gun thrust out.

'You'll join Severin in a cell,' he said glaring at Derrick. 'I'm sure he'll enjoy your company.'

Derrick's shoulders slumped, looking as if he'd surrender, but then with a double-take he scrambled for the door and while still struggling to keep his footing he barrelled out into the office. Simmons didn't shoot and so while Ralston glanced into the nearest cell at Severin, Hayward moved for the door.

'You'll stop right there,' Simmons said. 'I've had enough of the trouble you've brought to my town.'

Hayward looked at Ralston, who gave a brief nod and so with that, he ran for the jailhouse door with Ralston at his heels. Simmons still shouted at them to stop, but Hayward hurried across the office.

He gained the office door and swung out on to the boardwalk in time to see Derrick reach the bank. Derrick was sprinting and so by the time Hayward and Ralston had sped to a run, he'd reached the corner of the bank and swung to the side to disappear from view beside the music hall.

'Severin?' Hayward asked as he heard Simmons pounding after them.

'Derrick stabbed him,' Ralston said with a worried glance over his shoulder. 'But I reckon we interrupted him before he could finish him off.'

A thud sounded and Ralston grunted in pain before stumbling, making Hayward slide to a halt aiming to help him, but he saw that Simmons had tackled Ralston and he'd now flattened him to the boardwalk. With a growing hopeless feeling Hayward dismissed trying to help Ralston and he ran past the bank.

When he followed Derrick into the alley, his quarry was twenty paces ahead. He was looking over his shoulder with his brow furrowed as if in surprise that his pursuers weren't closer.

Hayward's arrival made Derrick concentrate on running and he rounded the corner of the music hall a few moments later. With his head down Hayward sprinted on although as he closed on the corner he glanced back.

He noted Simmons hadn't resumed the pursuit. Then he skidded round the corner before with a startled yelp of surprise he stopped and raised his hands.

Derrick was waiting at the corner and he'd trained his gun on him.

'Stay out of this,' Derrick said calmly. 'The last man I warned about getting involved with Malachi is now dead. I can't get distracted by trying to save a second man. And like Adam, if Ralston performs the bullet catch showdown tonight, he'll die.'

'How do you know this?'

Hayward waited for an answer, but Derrick looked past him. There was no sign of anyone else pursuing him, but Derrick backed away.

'Leave Malachi to me. I'll stop him.'

Derrick gave Hayward a long look and then sped up as he headed for the back door of the music hall. He stopped in the doorway to gesture at Hayward with his gun in an obvious command for him not to follow before he headed inside.

Hayward ignored the warning and he broke into a run reaching the doorway moments after Derrick had disappeared. The back of the stage was ten paces from the doorway and as Derrick had only just had enough time to reach there, he slowed in case Derrick had played the same trick on him again.

When he peered inside, the corridor and the part of the stage he could see were deserted. Bemused, he edged inside cautiously.

On stage and out of his view Malachi was talking with Florence, and his calm tone probably confirmed Derrick hadn't run past the stage. So Hayward edged forward until he saw that the steps leading on to the stage were standing askew.

He hurried to the steps where he glanced at Malachi and Florence to confirm they weren't paying him any attention before he knelt. He soon noted that the steps had been pushed aside to reveal the underside of the stage and so he slipped inside.

With only the light coming from the open entrance illuminating the area he could see little and so he moved forward cautiously. Three steps led down, which let him walk upright and when his eyes became accustomed to the gloom he moved more freely.

Work was being carried out down here as two heaps of dirt were piled up on the wooden floor, although he couldn't see a break in the flooring to show which area had been dug up. When he reached a point beneath the middle of the stage he stopped.

The thin outline of a rectangle of light was above him suggesting a trapdoor led up to the stage while the heaps were on either side of him. He could see into the corners and as there were no exits there, he turned round.

Derrick was kneeling in the entrance considering him.

'I can chase you around all day, but

you won't get away,' Hayward said.

'Perhaps I don't want to escape,' Derrick said with a smile. 'We're on the same side.'

'Prove it.'

'The proof is beneath your feet,' Derrick said. 'But if you figure it out, Malachi will kill you, so leave him to me.'

Derrick waited until Hayward started to ask for an explanation before he shoved the steps back into position with a scrape. When this left Hayward standing within the rectangle of light cast through the trapdoor, he looked up and sighed.

'I wonder how this trapdoor works,' he said to himself.

13

'I guess you saved Severin's life,' Sheriff Simmons said with a begrudging monotone voice.

'We may even have saved yours,' Hayward said.

'I know.' Simmons leaned back in his chair to consider them. 'And so, against my better judgement, you can perform the bullet catch showdown tonight.'

'Obliged,' Hayward and Ralston said together.

'Don't be. I've only agreed to that because letting you get shot up is quicker than running you out of town.'

Despite his comment, Hayward doubted that Simmons had much choice about letting the show go ahead.

After Malachi had heard him struggling to move the steps aside and had released him, Simmons had arrived. Derrick had gone, but Malachi had regained his usual confident demeanour and he had launched into a passionate plea for Simmons to let the show continue.

Simmons had been non-committal and so Malachi had urged Hayward and Ralston to spread the word that the show would go on even though Derrick was at large and determined to kill him. So by sundown, the town was abuzz with excitement putting Simmons in an impossible position.

With Hayward and Ralston spreading the word, Ralston hadn't had enough time to rehearse properly and neither had they found any sign of Derrick. So when Simmons left them, with only an hour before the audience arrived, they hurried back to the music hall to carry out the first full walk through of the act.

Bearing in mind that Derrick could have sneaked into the safe to kill Adam, Malachi positioned the safe in the centre of the stage towards the back.

This ensured nobody could sneak on to the stage from the sides unseen, although he placed it in front of the square area Hayward had noted when Derrick had trapped him beneath the stage. With the fake fortune being inside the safe, Derrick wouldn't be able to hide there if he took the bait and even better, Malachi reckoned that if Derrick tried to use the trapdoor, he would be seen from the stage.

Then Malachi moved on to talking Ralston through the things that could go wrong.

Despite Malachi's warnings, Hayward was confident that as the supposedly dangerous act was an elaborate trick, nothing should go wrong. His bigger concern was whether Derrick would try to disrupt proceedings, although as the last hour drifted away Ralston started dwelling on performing before an audience.

When Hayward joined Malachi's group in the back room, to his amusement Ralston paced around nervously making him wonder if he could cope with performing even if Derrick didn't try something.

No matter what encouragement he offered Ralston, his colleague ignored him. So he listened to the hubbub from the audience, which grew louder and more enthusiastic as the starting time approached.

Presently, the singer arrived on stage. Like last night she received catcalls, suggesting nobody was in the mood for seeing anything other than Malachi.

So she sang only three songs, but she fared better than the acrobats, who performed for only five minutes before they were booed off the stage. With that effective endorsement Malachi and Florence both nodded to Ralston before they headed off.

When loud and warm applause sounded, Ralston still didn't relax, leaving Hayward to sit back and watch him with a smile on his face as he wondered how he could put him at ease. In the end Ralston distracted himself by putting on his costume of a cloak and a mask and trying different postures to get the right enigmatic look.

When he was content with how he looked in costume, he shook hands with Hayward. Then without comment they left the back room and stood at the side of the stage in a position where they could watch proceedings as well as the audience.

As the back door was locked, Derrick shouldn't be able to get in. On the other hand, he had sneaked in last night to kill Adam without being seen.

With that thought Hayward headed around the back of the stage. On the other side, he noted the steps were still in place and when he moved them aside, the light shining down through the gaps in the stage let him see into all the corners.

Aside from the two heaps of dirt he saw nothing there and so heartened he came out and rejoined Ralston, who was standing stiffly as he apparently failed to conquer his nerves. Hayward murmured a few words of encouragement, and when Ralston didn't respond, he watched the act.

Malachi largely carried out the same act as Hayward had seen last night, although as many in the audience would have seen that performance, there were a few changes. Florence didn't appear from the safe at the start and she merely opened the door to display the treasure inside that someone would be offered later.

Then she scurried off while Malachi brought an audience member up on stage where he performed sleight of hand tricks. At first these were well-received, but the audience soon became restless.

Hayward presumed Severin's unavailability was limiting what Malachi could do and when Florence returned to the stage she whispered urgently to Malachi, as if something was amiss.

Before Hayward could work out what was troubling her, Malachi directed the man from the audience to stay and verify that everything was in order while giving Ralston the signal for him to come on stage.

Hayward patted Ralston on the back

and wished him well, which Ralston ignored as he headed off using a stiff-legged gait. While Malachi carried out the preliminaries, Hayward found a position where he could watch the audience for signs of trouble.

As it turned out, Florence was the first to appear concerned. When she left the stage to fetch the hoop through which they'd shoot, she directed a worried glance at him.

She moved on too quickly for him to ask her what was wrong, but when she returned from the back room, she dumped the hoop unceremoniously beside the stage.

'I was right to be worried,' she said with a concerned look at the stage before she urged Hayward to follow her. 'There's trouble.'

Hayward hurried after her and when he reached the back room, he soon saw what had concerned her. A man was lying face down beyond the door, his body blocking the doorway.

'Derrick?' Hayward asked as he

struggled to find a way to get into the room without standing on him.

'I didn't check,' Florence said. 'I heard a noise back here and when I went to fetch the hoop I found him.'

The hoop had been inside the room and so Hayward couldn't see why she'd brought it out while not checking on the man. He didn't waste time quizzing her and instead he stepped over the body, which let him identify the man.

'It's Ralston,' he murmured aghast.

He knelt beside him and turned him over, finding that he was breathing, although when he moved Ralston's head into a position where he could lie straight, he felt dampness on the back of his head.

'It looks like he was knocked out,' Florence said, standing behind him.

'But why?' Hayward looked Ralston's still form over until another worrying thought hit him making him look at the door. 'And if Ralston's in here, who's on the stage?'

His sudden movement let him see

Florence from the corner of his eye and clutched in her raised right hand was a spade. The moment she saw that he'd noticed her, she dashed the spade down.

In his shocked state Hayward reacted instantly and jerked his head aside. The dirty blade brushed his shoulder before the spade thudded down into the floor with a speed that dislodged it from Florence's hand while making her screech.

Hayward took advantage of her distress and grabbed her arm before throwing her forward. She went stumbling over Ralston's body, which made Ralston stir while she landed in a pile of Malachi's props sending them clattering down on her.

She lay gathering her strength before pushing the clothes and boards aside. When she turned she stayed hunched over and she considered him with contempt while flexing her jarred right hand.

'Like all the rest who come and go,

you don't know nothing,' she muttered.

'I don't know what you're angry about. We only wanted to stop Derrick harming you people ... ' Hayward trailed off as the obvious point hit him. 'Except Derrick didn't kill those women and neither did Severin. You did.'

She didn't retort to his guess and so he raised himself meaning to drag Ralston away, but the moment he put a hand to the door she kicked off from the floor and leapt at him.

As she'd been hunched over, she'd been able to keep the knife she'd held in her left hand hidden and with surprising dexterity, she swung the blade at his neck.

Even a glancing blow could prove fatal and so Hayward thrust up his right arm while jerking away from the blade. His forearm blocked her wrist a foot from his body and when she pressed against him, with his superior strength he kept the knife away with ease and then with his free arm he moved to grab her arm.

When she saw what he intended to do, she turned the knife in her grip and directed a stabbing motion at his head. The point sliced through the air six inches from his forehead, flashing reflected light into his eyes, but in that position he couldn't grab her arm and so she launched manic blows and then kicks at his chest and legs.

He absorbed the blows without difficulty while he waited for an opening that would let him use his strength against her. Her frantic attack forced him to take backwards steps to keep her knife hand away from his body and that walked him into the wall.

She kept moving and when that pressed their bodies up close, he lunged for her knife arm. She must have seen the intent in his eyes as she jerked backwards.

Then with a cry of defiance she twisted away from him to face Ralston and raised the knife high above her head.

Hayward saw what she intended to do. He pushed away from the wall as she put two hands to the knife and dropped to her knees making the knife swing down on a trajectory that would plunge the blade into Ralston's chest.

Heedless of his own safety, Hayward leapt at her, catching her around the shoulders from behind while the knife was still moving down.

They rolled over twice with their limbs entangled until they fetched up against the opposite wall. With her facing the wall, he gathered a tight grip of both her arms and held her rigidly, but she didn't fight back.

Then he felt sticky dampness on his hands and it was spreading. When he smelt the acrid tang of blood, he flexed his own body until he was sure he hadn't been hurt before he relaxed his grip to let her roll over on to her back.

The blade was buried deep into her stomach while both her hands clutched the knife, their combined weight having driven it home. Thoughts of the other women he'd found in other rooms ensured he didn't feel sympathy for her demise, and she helped to assuage his guilt when she sneered at him.

'You're too late,' she breathed. 'We've won.'

'What are you . . . ?' Hayward didn't bother completing his question as her eyes closed and she breathed out with a long sigh while slumping.

He held on to her, waiting for her to breathe in. When she didn't, he lay her down and moved on to Ralston, who was murmuring to himself as he came to.

As it would be a while before Ralston fully recovered and Florence was in no position to do him further harm, he left the room and headed back to the stage. He expected that with Florence having failed to return promptly with the hoop, Malachi would be struggling to hold the audience's attention, but he heard only silence ahead.

When he reached the edge of the stage, to his surprise the bullet catch showdown was going ahead. Two masked men were facing each other on either side of the hoop with their guns held downward.

The audience watched them with rapt attention while a woman stepped away from the safe and touched a lighted brand to the rope that surrounded the hoop. It took Hayward a moment to realize she was Florence.

As the flames skirted around the rope, Hayward did a double-take and he even looked towards the room where he and Florence had fought to convince himself he hadn't imagined their fight. Then he looked the woman over again.

She was wearing the same costume as Florence wore, but she had to be a different woman. That thought let him notice she was taller and stockier than the woman he'd fought with, but by then the flames had taken hold and the two masked gunmen were raising their guns.

Malachi was standing closest to him, which left him to wonder who the other masked man was if he wasn't Ralston.

'Derrick,' he said to himself.

14

'Stop this showdown,' Hayward demanded as he stepped out on to the stage.

Numerous audience members shouted in anguish. Then, as a more sustained roar of disapproval sounded from all corners of the music hall, Malachi's shoulders slumped as he appeared to struggle to turn the interruption into a part of the act.

With nobody else moving, Hayward walked on to claim the centre of the stage.

'What is the meaning of this rude interruption?' Malachi said when he found his voice. 'This act is dangerous beyond reason and it needs — '

'It's a lot more dangerous than you think,' Hayward shouted to be heard over the uproar as the front rows of the audience erupted from their seats and banged their fists on the stage. 'That's not Ralston and this is no trick.'

Malachi took a backward step. Figuring Derrick wanted to kill only Malachi, Hayward moved sideways to shield him, but Derrick stood impassively.

'Is that Derrick?' Malachi asked.

Hayward nodded and scrambling sounded as Malachi ran for safety, foregoing any attempt to retain his dignity. He ran to the front of the stage, but the wall of people pressing up against the edge made him skid to a halt.

Then he doubled back and sought to hide behind the safe. As the safe was made of thin wood, Hayward doubted it would shield him, but Derrick didn't follow him with his gun. Instead, he maintained his pose, which meant the gun was still aimed at Hayward.

'It's time to reveal everything,' Hayward said. 'I know you've not killed anyone and now everyone can know the truth.'

Derrick nodded, but the woman

stepped forward and screamed, her high-pitched shriek cutting through the hubbub and shocking everyone into silence.

'His gun's loaded and he's going to shoot,' she shouted, seemingly panic stricken. 'Stop him!'

Derrick started to shake his head, but a gunshot rang out from the audience, making Derrick drop to one knee clutching his side. Then he keeled over, his gun falling to the stage floor.

Hayward looked at the audience, seeing Sheriff Simmons had fired. People were spreading out to give him access to the stage.

Hayward hurried over to Derrick and rolled him over on to his back where he removed his mask to let him breathe easier, but his eyes were already glazing.

'You should have trusted me and told me the truth,' Hayward said.

'Malachi hides the truth in plain sight,' Derrick breathed. 'Nobody would have believed me.'

Derrick murmured some more, but

his voice wasn't strong enough for Hayward to hear him. Presently he silenced.

Hayward rocked back on his haunches and turned to the audience where Simmons had now reached the stage, but he was staring past Hayward with a hand raised in warning.

Hayward swirled round to find that the woman had claimed Derrick's gun and she'd turned it on him. With his hands raised Hayward got to his feet and backed away.

'Don't shoot,' he said. 'I'm not armed and I just want to help everyone explain what's happened.'

His last comment was for Simmons's benefit, but it was also the worst thing he could have said as it confirmed he knew what she and Florence had been doing.

'He attacked my sister,' the woman said. 'She's hurt backstage.'

'That's a good guess,' Hayward said. 'But it's not the way it happened and I'll gladly explain.'

Grumbling discontent grew in the audience making him wish he'd not retorted, as implying he'd hit a woman wasn't a sensible admission to have made.

The woman's eyes flared as she picked up on the prevailing sentiment and she raised the gun to aim at his chest.

'I hate to think what else he did to her,' she screeched. 'And what he planned to do to me.'

Several people shouted in anger. Then, with her pretence of ire making her face redden, she fired.

Hayward felt a dull pain in the chest, but it faded leaving with him a discomforting feeling as if he should be feeling pain, but wasn't.

'A wax bullet, after all,' Hayward said, tapping his chest.

She hurled the gun to the floor, her brow furrowing as she presumably thought quickly. With her standing still, Simmons clambered up on stage to join Hayward.

'I presume you can explain everything?' he said.

'I don't know what Derrick hoped to achieve with an unloaded gun, but it worked in the end.' Hayward pointed at the woman. 'Two women are in the act. While one woman is seen on stage by everyone, the other woman stays hidden. They use that bluff to kill in secret. You'll find the knife in the other woman's hand back stage.'

'No!' the woman shouted before running for the side of the stage.

She didn't reach it as a groggy looking Ralston arrived to block her path and scoop her up in his arms.

'Going somewhere, are we?' he asked.

The woman struggled, but when she failed to free herself from Ralston's arms, she relented, leaving Simmons to turn to the audience.

'I'll say this for the last time,' he declared. 'Nobody will perform the bullet catch showdown in Prudence again.'

This time nobody complained and when Simmons asked for the doors to be opened, people started filing out quietly. When Deputy Kennedy arrived, he was dispatched to the back room.

'I presume you'll now accept that Severin was innocent,' Malachi said when Kennedy had confirmed Hayward's tale.

'When I'm happy the sisters were behind the killings, he'll be free to go.' Simmons pointed at him. 'But I meant what I said. I never want to see this act in my town again.'

Malachi sighed and glanced around the stage, seemingly noting this was the last time he'd stand here.

'If that's the price of finally revealing the truth, so be it.'

Simmons nodded and with that, he escorted the woman away while Kennedy took care of Florence's body. When Malachi was left alone with Hayward and Ralston, Hayward gestured at the props.

'After we ruined your show, the least we can do is help you pack away.'

'That's not important. I'll deal with everything.'

Hayward moved to leave the stage,

but then he noticed the bloodstain where Derrick's body had lain. He turned back to Malachi.

'What do you reckon he wanted to achieve with a gun loaded with a wax bullet?'

'He wanted the truth to come out about my assistants and he needed an audience present to deliver it. He did that, but I doubt he expected you'd intervene or that Katherine and Florence would work out what he'd planned.'

Hayward frowned. 'Your stage shows have a habit of not going according to plan.'

Malachi put a hand to the safe as he prepared to move it off stage, but then he stopped and considered.

'Sadly you're right, and so perhaps this should be Malachi Muldoon's last performance anywhere, after all.'

★ ★ ★

'Apparently Katherine is Florence's sister,' Sheriff Simmons said when

Hayward and Ralston reported to the law office to answer the last of his questions. 'Not that she's being co-operative this morning.'

'But you released Severin so it must be clear they were behind everything?' Ralston said.

'It's clear, but it's not clear why she's so calm.'

Hayward couldn't provide an answer and so he and Ralston completed the details of what they knew about recent events and the past murders.

As Ralston knew more about the latter than Hayward did, he peered at the jailhouse door and wondered what had driven the sisters to kill so many women.

He and Ralston planned to head back to Bear Creek when Simmons dismissed them, and so he interrupted Ralston and pointed at the jailhouse.

'Perhaps while you're talking I might get an answer out of her,' he said.

Simmons shrugged, but he let him into the jailhouse. Katherine was the only prisoner and she was sitting in the cell in which Severin had been injured.

She considered him with her lips upturned slightly, as if she found the situation amusing and she settled back on her cot with her hands behind her head.

'I assume you have questions, too?' she said.

'And I assume you won't give me any answers either.'

She laughed. 'I enjoyed our brief time together. I'm sorry we didn't get to spend more time. If we had, I could have let you know I wasn't my sister.'

'And then you would have killed any woman I spoke to, like you did with Severin.'

Darkness clouded her features before she dismissed the matter with a wave of the hand.

'It wasn't that simple. Severin should have sided with us, not with Malachi. Then we wouldn't have had to punish those women.'

'Severin seemed to be a decent man,

so it's no surprise he didn't side with you.'

Katherine smiled, seemingly regaining her good humour.

'These questions must mean you don't know yet. I look forward to seeing the reaction.'

'Don't know about what?' He waited for an answer, but she clamped her lips tightly shut, making him back away towards the jailhouse door. 'I'll leave you. I hope you can keep your good humour through everything that'll happen to you.'

'I will.' She got off her cot and came to the front of the cell. 'I spent ten years learning the art of disappearing and of misdirection. Do you really think mere bars will hold me for long?'

Hayward considered responding to her taunt, but he heard raised voices in the law office, which made her chuckle, as if she'd expected this to happen. So Hayward headed back into the office.

Ralston was standing back to let a man Hayward hadn't met before explain something to Simmons, and the subject matter had shocked Simmons as he sported an incredulous expression. Then Simmons turned on his heels and hurried to the door with the newcomer hurrying along behind.

'What was that about?' Hayward asked.

'That was Vincent Cooper from the bank,' Ralston said. 'He says there's been a robbery.'

Hayward winced. 'Katherine knew some news was about to break. I assume that was it.'

Ralston joined Hayward in wincing and without further comment they hurried to the door. When they left the law office, Simmons was heading into the bank and so they hurried after him to find the bank was in turmoil with people scurrying about while others stood around talking in loud voices.

Nobody paid them attention and so they threaded their way through the throng until they found Simmons standing in the bank vault at the back. A safe stood in the middle of the room, it being the real version of the fake safe Malachi used in his act.

The door was open showing that the safe was empty. Behind the safe was a hole.

Simmons moved forward to peer into the hole. His posture confirmed it was deep and that a tunnel led away towards the music hall.

'Malachi must have dug the hole,' Simmons said.

'In three days?' Vincent said.

'Not days, years.'

Simmons and Vincent tipped back their hats in bemusement leaving Hayward to have the last word.

'And he is the master of hiding the truth in plain sight,' he said.

15

Hayward and Ralston caught their first sight of Malachi's wagon at sundown.

It stood beside a creek, looking as if Malachi had casually stopped to set up camp for the night, although as he had stolen the contents of Prudence's bank, it was unlikely that was his true intent. So he and Ralston drew back and observed the wagon, but even when Malachi and Severin merely pottered around the feeling grew that something was amiss.

Sheriff Simmons hadn't joined them in hurrying out of town after Malachi, preferring to stay and gather the full facts. His parting words were that a man who'd devoted years to robbing the bank by digging a tunnel from underneath the music hall stage whenever he performed would have his escape worked out and following his tracks wouldn't help.

When darkness had descended and only Malachi's campfire was lighting the terrain, Hayward shuffled closer to Ralston.

'Do you reckon we've been misdirected or not?' he asked.

'After everything that's happened I no longer have a clue,' Ralston said. 'But I guess there's only way to find out.'

Hayward grunted that he agreed and so moving stealthily they sneaked through the undergrowth towards the camp. Malachi was sitting beside the fire while Severin walked around awkwardly, suggesting he was moving to work off the stiffness in his side.

Hayward and Ralston kept their heads down until they reached the edge of an open area thirty yards from the fire where they knelt down. When Hayward looked up, Severin was no longer visible while Malachi had turned to look at the water.

With a nod to each other Hayward and Ralston agreed to wait until Severin came back into sight before they moved in on them, but long moments passed in which Severin didn't appear. Earlier he had been wandering aimlessly, but now they were closer to the fire, Hayward could see he must have been taking in the points from which someone could approach them.

Malachi's hunched posture gave Hayward the impression he might be nervous about them being followed. On the other hand, these men were masters of misdirection and Malachi was looking away from them, almost as if he'd turned his back on them to allay their suspicions . . .

Hayward swirled round, finding Severin standing over him, having sneaked up on them. While Ralston looked ahead, Severin kicked out, catching Hayward's gun and sending it hurtling into the undergrowth.

Hayward wrung his hand, but the effort involved in making the kick appeared to hurt Severin more than it hurt him as he clutched his side. So Hayward leapt to his feet and charged at Severin.

As Severin raised his gun, he ran into him, catching him in the chest with a leading shoulder, which with his stab wound made Severin screech in pain. His gun fell from his hand as Hayward ran him backwards until Severin tumbled over on to his back where he lay, clutching his ribs and groaning.

Hayward stood over him, but when Severin continued to bleat in pain, he concluded he didn't have any fight left in him and so he checked on how Ralston was faring. His colleague had stood up and he was holding a gun on Malachi, who was considering the scene with interest but without apparent concern.

'Watch Severin,' Hayward said. 'I'll deal with Malachi.'

Hayward waited until Ralston moved into the undergrowth and slapped a hand on Severin's shoulder before he looked for his gun. While keeping one eye on Malachi, he couldn't find it and so he settled for claiming Severin's gun before moving into the clearing.

'Release Severin,' Malachi said with calm authority as Hayward approached.

'You two aren't getting away.' Hayward stopped twenty yards from Malachi. 'This ends here.'

Malachi was wearing a cloak and he fiddled with the tie around his neck until he approved of the way the cloak hung about his body. Then he considered Hayward, who settled his own stance, although he held his gun aimed downwards.

'Your pursuit ends here. Our new life is about to begin. The show is no more and if you don't throw down your gun, you will be, too.'

'I talked to Katherine. She was arrogant, too, except she's now in a cell, as you will be.'

'A cell won't hold her for long and I'll never have to be in one. I am Malachi Muldoon, the greatest — '

'Enough of the boasts.'

Malachi shrugged. 'You must allow me to enjoy a feeling of satisfaction. I've been coming to Prudence for ten years and — '

'You've been going there for three years. You took over the magic show from Jubal Jackson after he died on stage.'

'I didn't take over Jubal's show and he didn't die.' Malachi laughed. 'In fact Jubal never even existed.'

Malachi twitched, making his cloak swirl as he invited Hayward to make the connection.

'You were Jubal Jackson until you became Malachi Muldoon, but people didn't notice because they saw you only once a year and then they were busy watching your assistants. But why?'

'In towns where we'd performed before, people were asking too many questions about the bodies. So Jubal died, but the best magicians know how to make people reappear and a year later he was reborn.'

'And each year you secretly dug a little further, while getting everyone used to seeing your fake safe filled with fake money.' Hayward watched Malachi nod. 'Your planning was meticulous, but it wasn't perfect, or else Derrick wouldn't have nearly killed you.'

'He came close, but he played into my hands.' Malachi chuckled. 'While everyone looked for my prospective killer, nobody worried about a robber, and with my murderous assistants doing their worst, he added colour to an already fraught situation.'

'You stood by and let them kill innocent women,' Hayward spluttered, aghast. 'And they killed Adam, too, just to take attention away from what you were really doing!'

'Don't look so shocked. That's what I do. I'm the master of — '

'You're the master of deception, I know, and you'll pay for that.'

'Except I won't.' Malachi raised a finger. 'Remember, I killed nobody, the sisters did.'

Malachi's lack of guilt made Hayward shake his head and in response, Malachi lowered his finger. Hayward watched his hand, aware that Malachi would try to deceive him and sure enough, in a blur of motion that Hayward couldn't follow, Malachi swirled his cloak with his other hand.

When the cloak stopped moving, Malachi was clutching a gun, although he held it aimed downwards.

'So we have a showdown.' Hayward raised his gun a mite as he regained his composure. 'Except I'm familiar with the reality while you're only familiar with the fantasy.'

'Do you really think you can defeat a man who can catch a bullet with his teeth?'

Malachi shrugged, spreading his cloak and ensuring it didn't impede him, although he puffed his chest, inviting Hayward to take a shot at him.

'No man can do that and live.'

Malachi chuckled and adopted the stance he'd taken on stage with his arms thrust backwards and his head jutting forward, as if preparing to snatch the bullet from the air with his teeth.

'I am the great Malachi Muldoon. I defy death nightly, and I defy you to do your worst.'

Hayward sighed with irritation deciding he didn't know or care what Malachi was trying to achieve. He waved a dismissive hand at him before cautiously moving forward with his gun aimed at his chest.

'Keep your hands still and don't make any more sudden moves.'

'I don't intend to make any sudden moves. The bullet catch requires extreme concentration.'

Malachi's tone was so commanding that Hayward stopped. He considered him, noting that even though Malachi could move his hands quickly, it would take time to turn his gun on him. Then he glanced around, wondering what surprises Malachi might have planned.

He saw nothing to concern him.

Darkness surrounded the wagon and Ralston had Severin under control, although Severin was now stirring.

Hayward moved on to stand ten paces from Malachi, the distance over which the bullet catch showdown would have been enacted.

'I don't know what you hope to get out of this posturing, but don't force me to kill you.'

'You won't. Aim true and I'll catch the bullet with my teeth.' Malachi glanced at Hayward's gun. 'And that means you have to aim higher than my chest.'

An exasperated Hayward moved on, eager to end Malachi's game, but behind him Ralston grunted and scuffling footfalls sounded. He looked over his shoulder to see Severin had regained his strength and he and Ralston were tussling over Ralston's gun.

Severin had put two hands to Ralston's wrist, but Ralston was keeping his arm still without difficulty and so he turned back to find Malachi was slowly swinging his gun arm forward.

The moment Malachi saw his attention was back on him, he jerked his arm upwards.

Hayward fired making Malachi grunt in pain. Malachi looked him in the eye, his expression one of shock, perhaps because Hayward hadn't succumbed to his mind games.

Malachi conceded he'd been bettered with a nod. His gun fell from his grasp before he keeled over to lie face down in the dirt.

Ralston was still holding the wounded Severin at bay without difficulty and so Hayward hurried to Malachi and turned him over on to his back. Malachi flopped down with a hand clutched to his chest.

'I didn't want to do that,' Hayward said.

He thought Malachi wouldn't respond, but Malachi cranked open an eye to consider him.

'A good magician is only as good as his assistant,' he murmured. 'And you're terrible.'

Hayward smiled, but Malachi didn't

appear to notice as his eyes became unfocussed. Hayward reached out, meaning to confirm Malachi was dead, but a thud sounded behind him.

He swirled round to be faced with the sight of Severin reeling away having received a swinging punch to the jaw. As Severin lost his footing and slammed down on his back, Hayward moved away from Malachi and hurried back to the undergrowth.

When he joined Ralston, his colleague didn't use his advantage, as Severin was lying slumped and still. While Ralston fingered his jaw, Hayward checked on Severin and found that when he'd fallen, he had knocked his head on a rock and this time he was unconscious.

They took a leg apiece and dragged Severin into the clearing to lie alongside Malachi. Then they moved on to the wagon.

'One man captured and one man dead,' Ralston said approvingly. 'And we've reclaimed the stolen money.'

Hayward nodded, although as he clambered into the wagon, he still glanced at Malachi's body in irritation, as the full story of his activities had probably died with him.

The safe containing the money was lying on its side and so Ralston used Malachi's spade to lever open the door. He peered beneath it and then with an irritated grunt he moved so he could use the available moonlight.

'Anything wrong?' Hayward asked after Ralston had shuffled into several positions without finding one that was to his liking.

'I'm not sure.'

Ralston reached inside the safe, rooted around, and withdrew a bar. Even in the poor light Hayward could see it was wood that had been painted gold.

They both winced and without further comment they dragged the safe to the back of the wagon. With the safe moving with greater ease than it should do if it was loaded down with money, they wasted no time examining it further and instead they tipped it over the side.

The safe clattered to the ground and the thin wood shattered spilling more gold-coloured bars, bundles of cut-up newspaper and gaudy glass jewels on to the ground.

'Tricked,' Hayward muttered.

'I knew we found them too easily.'

Hayward jumped down and kicked bars aside.

'At least Malachi didn't profit from . . .' He trailed off and looked at Ralston, who winced before jumping down and seeing if the obvious thought that had just hit Hayward was in fact true.

Ralston peered around the end of the wagon and then came back to face Hayward.

'We have been tricked,' he said simply. 'Severin's still there, but Malachi's gone.'

With an angry roar Hayward kicked the remnants of the safe, breaking the largest piece into two and sending the parts flying away before he joined

Ralston in heading over to where Malachi's body had fallen. Any hopes that the worst hadn't happened fled when they discovered the ground around the spot was unmarked.

Severin was still out cold, so he hadn't dragged Malachi's body away. Malachi had walked away on his own.

'He must have planned this and we played into his hands.'

'But how? No man can catch a bullet.'

'No man can catch a real bullet.'

Hayward drew his gun and examined the chambers. He didn't need to explain what he found there other than to wipe the wax off his fingers on to his jacket.

'Severin made sure you swapped guns.' Ralston considered and then slapped his forehead. 'That's another one of Malachi's tricks. We couldn't work out why Derrick confronted Malachi with an unloaded gun, except he didn't know it was unloaded because Malachi had swapped it.'

'Malachi planned to feign his own death again, like he did when he was Jubal Jackson. He failed, but Katherine didn't know that and she incriminated herself.' Hayward frowned. 'And he'd have failed here if you'd taken him on instead of me.'

Ralston shrugged. 'With Malachi, you always pick the card he wants you to pick. And like all good magicians, he can disappear, too.'

Hayward looked around, wondering in which direction Malachi had fled. He would probably have left a horse near by along with the stolen money, and as he must have planned his escape well, Hayward didn't fancy his chances of finding him.

'You tricked us,' he shouted, his voice echoing in the distance. 'But you'll never profit from your escapade. We have Severin. You double-crossed him and left him to answer for everything. He'll be angry and he'll tell us your secrets. You'll never remain free.'

He waited until the last echo faded

and turned to Ralston, who smiled and patted him on the back.

'And if Severin doesn't talk, no matter how long it takes, we'll make Malachi pay.'

Hayward nodded. 'Magicians can disappear into thin air, but one day they have to come back, and we'll be waiting for him.'

16

One year later . . .

'It's a trick,' Bathsheba said.

'Of course it is,' Hayward said with a bored tone. 'That's why it's called a magic show.'

Bathsheba frowned, but Hayward doubted that would stop her continuing to point out how Professor Prometheus Pomeroy, the world's most exciting practitioner of the secret arts, would next deceive his audience.

Although Hayward had needed a way to cover his true intent while he was in Beaver Ridge, he already regretted accompanying a saloon girl who had seen the show the previous night, albeit on her own.

Bathsheba had already sneered at Prometheus's first trick in which he'd opened a previously empty box only to find his female assistant Geraldine inside dressed in a sparkly costume. Bathsheba had pointed out a square shape on the safe wall that suggested a second door.

Hayward had ignored her and he'd had to ignore her again when she'd explained her theory about how Prometheus had discovered a card behind Geraldine's ear. This was the same card that an audience member had identified earlier even though Prometheus had burnt the pack.

She reckoned Prometheus had two packs of cards and Geraldine had told him which card had been chosen. Hayward gritted his teeth as he prepared to ignore her prattle, but then Prometheus moved on to the main part of the act.

This was the only part he was interested in. It was the part he'd watched carefully last night, as well as studying it in the three previous towns in which Prometheus had performed.

'And now,' Prometheus announced from the front of the stage while facing the lively audience, 'for your edification and delight I will perform the most exciting act you'll ever witness in your entire lives.'

Prometheus waited while the audience applauded and shouted encouragement.

'Many magicians have performed the bullet catch and many have died,' he continued. 'Undeterred, some have even increased the danger with tricks such as staging a bullet catch showdown. But I won't be performing a trick here tonight. I'll take my life into my own hands by catching a bullet fired by one of you.'

The audience provided an appreciative murmur and so Prometheus set about selecting three random members of the audience to take part.

Hayward had observed this selection process and he'd learnt just how random it really was and just who he had to bribe to participate.

The next ten minutes proceeded as usual with Prometheus bantering with members of the audience and, when they didn't meet his exacting standards, refusing them permission to participate.

His screening process generated grumbling complaints from the audience and so when the fifth man stood up, he picked him without questioning him.

Hayward didn't know who this man was, but he also knew the first man to be picked never got to perform in the rest of the act.

Bathsheba proved her worth when she leapt to her feet and cried out for Prometheus to pick her escort. Prometheus did as she asked and he engaged in lively banter with her without casting Hayward even a cursory glance.

Prometheus completed his choices by picking out the only man who had stood up at the back of the audience. This man kept his hat lowered so Malachi couldn't see he was Ralston Hope.

While Geraldine took the three men aside and dressed them in masks and cloaks while explaining what they had to do, Prometheus set up the stage.

Ten minutes later the three men were led back to a stage that looked the same as it had done last year when Hayward had first seen the act in Bear Creek. A glass-filled hoop separated the gunman from his target, while the new safe stood to the side.

The only change was that the three masked men were lined up before Prometheus and he built up the tension by selecting one of them to shoot at him by asking them to draw cards.

Hayward stood in the centre, which meant he would pick the high card. When this happened, as it had done every time he'd watched the act before, he nodded to the masked Ralston, who had lost the fair game of chance they had conducted the previous night.

With Ralston picking the second highest card, Geraldine presented him with a shining Peacemaker on a tray for him to examine. Ralston grabbed the tray with his left hand while he nervously rooted around for the gun with his shaking right hand.

He was supposed to remove the gun from the tray and check it was loaded, so Geraldine held on to the tray. This led to an awkward moment where they both strained until Ralston's apparent nervousness tipped the tray over, spilling the gun on to the floor.

Ralston apologized profusely and generally got in the way as he swooped down on the gun, which disappeared beneath his cloak for a moment before he rescued it and stood up.

With a hand to the chest Ralston mimed stilling his rapidly beating heart. Then he checked the gun was loaded before returning it to the tray.

Ralston backed away leaving Hayward to claim the gun, which he did quickly before anyone noticed it wasn't the gun Geraldine had presented to Ralston originally.

'What's your name?' Prometheus asked when he faced Hayward through the hoop.

'I'd prefer not to give one,' Hayward said, speaking rapidly and apparently nervously to disguise his voice. 'I'm worried this will go wrong because I sure don't reckon nobody can catch a bullet with his teeth.'

Prometheus adopted his usual posture with his head jutted forward and his arms thrust back. Then he thought better of it and straightened up to address the audience.

'My new friend's concern is valid. What I do here tonight is dangerous beyond reason. So I state before all you good people that if my death-defying act goes awry and I am killed on this very stage, no blame will be laid at the feet of my killer.'

Prometheus gave a short bow and Hayward accepted his order with a nod. Prometheus then waited until the audience quietened before he adopted his pose again.

Hayward rolled his shoulders and raised the gun.

'I'm pleased you said that, because I've heard a magician is only as good as his assistant.' Hayward aimed at Prometheus's head through the glass-filled hoop. 'And I fear I'm not a very good one, Malachi.'

Hayward waited until Prometheus blinked with surprise. Then he fired.

The mining town of King Creek sits in the heart of the Nevada goldfields. It has no law to speak of but Stover's Law — ruthlessly enforced by one greedy woman, her three callous sons, and a dozen hired gunmen. The Stover family is systematically fleecing the townsfolk of everything they have, with anyone standing in their way either bought off — or killed off. In desperation, Pearl Denton turns to her old friend, legendary town-tamer Sam Judge, for help . . .

SAVAGE

Jake Henry

In 1864, Captain Jeff Savage is tasked with taking down Carver's Raiders, a ruthless bunch of killers who have blasted a bloody path through the Shenandoah Valley. The mission is a failure, and Carver escapes with a handful of men. Two years later, he and his gang rob a bank in Summerton, murdering Savage's wife Amy. Several outlaws escape in the aftermath: armed with their names, Savage sets out to track each one down and exact his revenge . . .

THE SHOESTRINGERS

C. J. Sommers

Benjamin Trout, foreman of the K/K Ranch, has been cut loose for being too old — while Eddie 'Dink' Guest, a new hire, has been fired for being too young. With nowhere to go, both ride out together to seek work elsewhere. When they encounter widowed Beth Robinson and her daughter Minna in the wilderness, they are invited back to the women's ranch — and become the Robinsons' allies in the struggle to save their land from the predatory Cyrus Sullivan.

DEAD MAN DRAW

Walt Keene

Retired lawman Dan Shaw and veteran gunfighter Tom ride into the sprawling town of Dead Man Draw. Quickly hired as sheriff and deputy, and charged with collecting protection money from town businesses, it doesn't take long to discover why their appointments were so hasty — the place is crawling with hired killers, and two drifters are considered expendable. But these old-timers have an ace in the hole — their friend Wild Bill Hickok has their backs . . .

PROFESSOR HAYES

Billy Moore

'Professor' A.J. Hayes is hired to serve as a teacher in San Juan, where he manages to upset the community by not only instantly wedding Rachel McNew — a young woman arriving on a marriage train — but disciplining the son of Curt Tucker, the local mine owner, and brawling with Tucker in public. Fired from the school, A.J. and Rachel — still happily married despite everything — move to a cabin in a valley. But their new life together is soon under threat . . .

TOOTS McGEE

J. W. Throgmorton

Toussaint 'Toots' William McGee is riding a trail when he suddenly topples from his saddle, shot. On recovering consciousness, he finds himself staring into the barrel of a rifle. Sarah Baxter has ambushed him, having mistaken him for Tom Danton, the man who killed her family. Upon realising her error, she takes Toots to her home to recuperate, where he learns of her family's plight — and pledges to assist with their struggle against Danton and his murderous master Web Griffin . . .